Not A Chance

Not A Chance

MICHELLE MULDER

ORCA BOOK PUBLISHERS

Library and Archives Canada Cataloguing in Publication

Mulder, Michelle, 1976-
Not a chance / Michelle Mulder.

Issued also in electronic formats.
ISBN 978-1-4598-0216-2

I. Title.
PS8626.U435N68 2013   jC813'.6   C2012-907456-X

First published in the United States, 2013
Library of Congress Control Number: 2012952943

Summary: Dian is outraged when her fourteen-year-old Dominican friend
announces that she is engaged to be married.

*Orca Book Publishers is dedicated to preserving the environment and has printed
this book on Forest Stewardship Council® certified paper*

Orca Book Publishers gratefully acknowledges the support for its publishing programs
provided by the following agencies: the Government of Canada through the Canada Book
Fund and the Canada Council for the Arts, and the Province of British Columbia through
the BC Arts Council and the Book Publishing Tax Credit.

Cover design by Teresa Bubela
Cover photo by iStockphoto.com
Author photo by David Lowes

ORCA BOOK PUBLISHERS   ORCA BOOK PUBLISHERS
PO Box 5626, Stn. B   PO Box 468
Victoria, BC Canada   Custer, WA USA
V8R 6S4   98240-0468

www.orcabook.com
Printed and bound in Canada.

16 15 14 13 • 4 3 2 1

For Maia

One

"You're here!" I sit straight up in my metal bunk bed, yank at the mosquito netting and wrestle my way out.

Aracely stands in the doorway, laughing at me. "Of course I'm here. I live here, remember? *You're* the one who takes off at the end of every summer, Dian."

I ignore that comment and zigzag between suitcases and boxes to hug her. She doesn't have to know that I didn't want to come this year. She's the only person who might make this summer bearable, and I don't want to hurt her feelings.

She kisses my cheeks, tucks her black hair behind one ear and surveys my baggy, tie-dyed shorts and red polka-dot blouse. "It will never get better, will it?"

I clench my teeth and shake my head. The clothes are one of the reasons I didn't want to come. Every summer, my parents bring suitcases full of donated stuff to wear while we're here and leave behind when we go. The outfits are almost always awful, and they're never anything I'd choose. This spring, when I realized that my parents weren't going to let me stay home with my grandmother while they came here, I lobbied for them to at least let me bring my own clothes to wear. (They're secondhand too, because according to my parents, buying brand-new clothes exploits poor workers in other countries and impacts the environment. But at least in Canada I get to choose my own clothes.) Mom asked if I planned to leave most of my own clothes behind at the end of the summer, and when I said no, she and Dad looked at me like I was dumping toxic waste into the village stream. They gave me a long lecture on compassion being more important than vanity. I shot back that they should have some compassion for me for once. They hit the roof, and here I am, at the end of June, in polka dots and tie-dye. At least they promised not to take any pictures of me this summer. That's their grand gesture at understanding what it's like to be me.

Aracely shakes her head. "If you were my size, I'd give you half my clothing. You know that, don't you?"

I smile because I know she's trying to help. Last summer, out of pity, she dressed me up like the other girls our age in Cucubano, in a tight pink top and a short skirt. She said I looked hot, but I felt like a Barbie gone horribly wrong—too tall, too flat, too skinny. Aracely is only a year older than me, but she has curves in all the right places, and at fourteen she could pass for sixteen.

The only sad thing is that big scar on her cheek. A donkey bit her when she was four, and someone stitched it up for her, but not well. It's not like people here get free plastic surgery after an accident like they do in Canada. The scar takes up most of her cheek—a jagged line, rough around the edges where the donkey's teeth scraped over the skin before biting through.

The first time I saw her, I was terrified. Then again, at five I was terrified of most things, and it didn't help that my parents had brought me to a tiny settlement in the Dominican Republic where the ground was orange and everyone lived in wooden huts and spoke a language I didn't understand. I remember hiding behind my mother in the schoolyard, with all the local mothers and their kids watching us. The adults were smiling at each other, and the kids stared at me, wide-eyed. My mother had a firm hand on my shoulder to keep me from bolting, and her grip tightened when the little girl with the horrible scar marched over to me. The girl took a pink hibiscus flower from behind her ear and placed it behind mine, then took my hand and led me off to play. She taught me how to pick the sweetest oranges, where to find the best climbing trees and how to catch a butterfly. Along the way, she taught me Spanish.

The priest who invited my parents here hired Aracely's mother to do our laundry, cook our meals and look after me. I spent most of that first summer at Aracely's house, and that suited me just fine; I loved feeling like part of a big family. As we got older, Aracely and I would take off on adventures of our own. My parents would assume I was with Aracely's mom, and Aracely's mom would assume I was fine because

I was with Aracely. It worked out great, because no one would have let us do half of what we did if we'd actually asked permission.

"Sorry I couldn't meet the truck when you got here," Aracely says now, smoothing her skirt. "*Abuela* needed to find *periquito* for my sister's cramps. Abuela was convinced that some still grows over by Beto's field, but it doesn't, and by the time she believed me, we were too far away to get back before the *aguacero*, and we had to wait until the rain stopped."

"No worries," I lie. I'm not going to tell her how I freaked out when I didn't see her with everyone else. A lot can happen here between summers, and it's not like she and I can text each other our news. Even if my anti-cell-phone parents would let me have one, Cucubano doesn't have cell reception. Or reliable electricity. Every time we come back here, we have no idea who's been born or died since the summer before, and this afternoon Aracely's mom must have seen the panic on my face, because she cut through the crowd to tell me my friend was only away for the morning.

I should have guessed, of course. Aracely and her grandmother—her abuela—often take off on expeditions to find some plant or another. Her abuela is a healer, and Aracely is learning. Last summer, Dad saw some of Aracely's drawings of medicinal plants and asked her family if she could come to Canada to study someday. He says that with her knowledge of traditional medicine, she could make a great academic career for herself and then come back here and really help the community. Her parents were thrilled. Aracely is terrified, but she's willing to do it if it'll help. Now that's courage. She's never even been as far as Ocoa, the closest city, a two-hour bus ride away, but in a few years she'll be living in Canada, which is so different from here that it might as well be on another planet.

"Do you want help putting stuff away?" Aracely scans my family's makeshift bedroom. Before we arrived, Aracely's mom cleaned it within an inch of its life. The concrete floor shone, the bunk beds were made up as well as any hotel's, the chalkboards were a spotless black, and not a speck of dust remained on the teacher's desk shoved into the corner. (It's like this every summer. Being invited here by the priest in Ocoa means people treat our arrival like a royal visit.) In just a few hours, my parents and I have managed to track in big clumps of the inevitable orange dirt, and we've strewn our things all over the place.

I should clean up. Mom and Dad are in the other classroom, unpacking boxes for their summer medical clinic, and I came back here to organize but decided to take a nap instead—not that I had much success. Whoever thinks roosters only crow at dawn has never met Rafael's roosters, and why our neighbor has to keep his snorting pigs and braying donkey right outside our window is beyond me. If I were at home this summer, I could sleep whenever I wanted—not that I would, of course. I'd be working at the bike shop, or lying on the beach, or going to the movies with Emily. In other words, doing what any normal Canadian teenager has the right to do in the summertime. Unless you've got parents like mine, who expect you to spend every waking moment saving the world.

"The mess can wait," I tell Aracely. "Let's go somewhere."

"To the river," she says.

"Yes!" I flip open a suitcase to find my bathing suit. Two years ago, Aracely announced that she was too old to swim in the river. I thought that was hilarious, since she was only twelve, but she said, *I've got boobs. I get my period. I'm a woman now, and respectable women don't run around half naked and jump in the river. That's for boys and* marimachos.

I asked her what a marimacho is. It means something like "butch woman" and is a big insult. No matter how much she tried to stop me from swimming, I kept doing it. She stayed on the shore while I swam. "So glad you've come to your senses about the swimming thing," I say now. "How can you live so close to a fantastic river and not swim in it?"

"I don't, and I won't." She leans back against the bunk bed, arms crossed. "I have to get some *berro*, and I'm asking you along."

Berro. I rack my brain, trying to remember what that is. Every year, between summers, I forget way too much Spanish. A few times at home, my parents tried to speak it with me to keep theirs up, but it just felt silly. But when we're here, they insist that I speak Spanish, no matter what. I spend the start of each summer rummaging for words I used to know or trying to understand things I probably understood the year before.

I think berro is a little, flat-leaved plant that grows in clusters by the river. Aracely's abuela collects it for one of her remedies.

I unearth my swimsuit and stand up. "I'll let my parents know where we're going."

"I already told them." Aracely links her arm with mine, pushes open the door and leads me into the sunshine. A dozen kids are playing in front of the school, on a patch of ground just big enough for a game of catch. Adults lounge along the wall, talking with each other or calling to my parents, who try to arrange boxes and socialize at the same time. The day we arrive is always like this, with everyone stopping by to say hello. Every other day is pretty similar too. The school is smack in the middle of the settlement, and anyone going anywhere usually stops in to chat.

"Come on." Aracely tugs on my arm. "Let's go. It's not just berro I want. I want privacy. I've got something important to tell you."

Two

All the way down the long orange-dirt road to the river, she keeps me in suspense. "Too many people around," she says, which would seem funny to anyone who doesn't know Cucubano.

By the looks of it, this road cuts through virgin jungle. Two kilometers down the hill, by the river, a minivan or *guagua* goes by twice a day, bringing people to nearby villages. But on this particular road, the priest's pickup truck that brought us here was probably the first vehicle in a week, and it might be the last for the next month. Still, if you look closely, you'll see small gaps in the plants—narrow footpaths that lead to little huts where people live. Houses here are small, and families are big.

Lots of families of eight live in one room, and until someone pops out of the bush and onto the road, you'd never guess they were here.

About thirty families live on this hill. Everyone knows everything about everyone, and anything overheard on the road is fair game for gossip. I remember the summer I walked down to the river with my mother and admitted I was constipated. I knew she wouldn't tell anyone, yet within days the whole village was talking about my blocked bowels, and seven women came by with home-made remedies.

So I can understand why Aracely won't mention anything until we get to the river, where the sound of the water will drown out our whispers and we'll be able to see anyone who might be listening in. What I don't understand is why we're going to the river if she's not going to swim. She could pick berro another time, and we could go to last summer's hideout instead. It's a lot closer.

A few weeks before I left last year, she took me to her uncle's old house. He left it behind, along with his tomato field, when he moved to the city. Aracely said no one was using it, so we cleared away the vines and the bugs, swept out the dust, brought bottles of water and food, and spent most of our free time there, talking about things we didn't dare say aloud anywhere else. I told her all about life in Canada. I ranted about how my parents never focus on good things and only see what needs improvement. Aracely ranted about how her mother wants to start her own business but never does and how her father can never save money because he is always giving it to his drunken older brother. In our hideout, I felt closer to Aracely than I'd ever felt to anybody.

"What happened to our hideout?" I ask her now, and for some reason Aracely looks surprised.

"Oh, it's still there," she says, avoiding my eyes. "I'd just rather go to the river."

I imagine the place is covered in vines again. It's a shame, but it's not like I expected Aracely to keep it all clean until I got back. We have a whole summer ahead of us to clean it up anyway. Before I can ask any more about it, though, she asks about Emily, my best friend back home.

"Oh, she's fine," I say. "My parents don't want me hanging around her so much anymore though."

Emily loves buying clothes, and my father thinks she's vain. (More specifically, he complains about her "corruptive consumer mentality." Like hanging out at the mall makes her the devil's spawn. I don't explain any of this to Aracely, because how do you explain consumerism to someone whose family barely has money for food and who's never heard of malls?) "Emily's gorgeous, and she's totally in love with this guy at our school," I tell Aracely. "Not that she ever talks to him though."

"Of course not," Aracely says. "She can't show too much interest."

I blink. How is it that every other girl my age seems to know these things, and I don't have a clue about them? A guy talks to me, and I get tongue-tied. I don't know how I'll ever figure out what to say and when to say it. "I just don't get it. How will Cody know she likes him if they never speak?"

Aracely frowns. "You mean, he doesn't speak to her either? Not even when he brings her flowers, or dances with her?"

"He doesn't do those things," I say. "He doesn't know she exists."

Aracely waves a hand like she's swatting Cody away. "What does Emily see in him? No one should go for a guy who can't tell right off how amazing she is."

I wonder what Emily would say to that—or what Emily would say to Aracely about anything, for that matter. I can't imagine the day they meet. Emily's as shy as Aracely's outspoken. Sometimes I can hardly believe I'm friends with two such different people. But that's what my life is like. The person I am in Canada has nothing to do with who I am here.

At home, I'm the serious kid. The one who was on the debating team, the president of the Enviro Club and a founding member of Kids 4 Social Justice. Even though I quit all that, kids at school still think of me as a freak. No cell phone. No new clothes ever. No dreams of driving one day, because bicycles and buses are the only vehicles my parents believe in. (When we fly, my parents get rid of their guilt by paying for thousands of trees to be planted somewhere in the world and by spending weeks telling me that the potential good of our trip outweighs the environmental destruction that our flights will cause.) Here in Cucubano, I'm the childish kid. The marimacho. Every other thirteen-year-old girl is making meals, sewing, cleaning and looking after brothers and sisters. I'm the only one who wants to climb trees, swim in the river, chase fireflies and watch the clouds roll by. If I'd stayed home this summer, Grandma wouldn't have cared how many movies I went to or how many times I hung out with Emily at the mall. She knows that's what normal Canadian teenagers do, and she knows that the only way I'll ever be allowed to do that is if I'm in Canada while my parents are running a medical clinic in a different country. But here I am, in a place I'll never belong.

We round the last curve before reaching the main road. "You sure you're not going to swim?" I ask.

"Nah," Aracely says. "I'm not a kid anymore."

I shrug. "Neither am I, but I still like swimming in the river."

She says nothing at first. Across the narrow strip of pitted pavement, a toddler in a grubby T-shirt and a diaper waves at us from outside a wooden hut. We wave back, and he runs screeching to the nearby cookshack. The smell of sautéed garlic is making me hungry.

"It's different for you," Aracely says. "People don't mind so much what you do."

Because you're foreign. That's the part she doesn't add, because she knows it would sting. We talked about this last summer, when I told her I didn't feel like I fit in here anymore.

"For a while, it was the same with me," Aracely continues. "People made exceptions, and they didn't mind me hanging out with you and doing what you did."

I frown at her. "What are you talking about? You were born here. Everyone in your family was born here."

"You know what I mean." She waves at her scar. She's told me before that her family has been less strict because they feel sorry for her. That must be what she's talking about now.

We walk a few meters along the paved part of the road—not a car in sight—and step onto a trail between the bushes that leads down to the river. The berro grows in low green patches where the water meets the shore. Aracely doesn't stick to this side of the river though. She takes off her worn, pink flip-flops and wades across to a little island in the middle. The water moves too fast for berro to grow there, but we can see anyone who comes along, and the current will drown out our words.

I flop down on a big rock. "So what's the news?"

My friend's face splits into a grin. "I'm getting married."

I gape at her. She smiles back, a shy smile, like she can't believe her luck. My eyes flicker down to her flat stomach, and she swats me. "No, not yet, Dian. What kind of a girl do you think I am?"

Not one who would be happy about getting married at fourteen, I want to shout, but I can't get the words out. Her smile falters a bit and her eyes dart to the side, as though maybe we should ditch this conversation and look for berro after all. "I'm sorry about your dad's plans," she says. "I mean, I know he wanted to help and everything, and it was good to know I had an option if I couldn't find anyone who…"

She keeps talking, but I'm not hearing her anymore. An *option*? It wasn't an option. It was a future. A future way better than getting married at fourteen. And now she's throwing it away?

Aracely's staring at me, waiting for me to say something.

"Who?" I blurt out. "I mean, who's the groom?" I trip over the last word.

I know it won't be a stand-up-in-church kind of wedding—the priest hardly ever comes here, so weddings are basically big parties and then the couple moves in together—but people still talk about brides and grooms. No one has any papers to say they're man and wife, but everyone in the village acts as *padrinos*, or godparents, of the marriage. No one doubts its officialness.

"He lives on the other side of the hill. His name's Vincente—Vin for short." Aracely uses the same hushed whisper that Emily uses when she talks about Cody. "He's not like other guys around here. He's going to be somebody. When my uncle came to visit a few months ago, he told Vin about a mine near Santo Domingo. Vin figures if he works there for a year, he'll have enough money to build a house here, so he left for Santo Domingo a few weeks ago. Before he went, he asked *Papá* if we could marry!"

"And your father went along with it?"

"Of course!" Aracely snaps. "We just haven't told anyone yet because we're waiting to hear that Vin has a job. A year at the mine, and he'll be able to get some land and help Papá with the farm. Why *wouldn't* we get married?"

"For a thousand reasons!" I say. "Because you're only fourteen. Because you barely know him. Because you could study in North America and never have to worry about money again."

Aracely stands up and brushes off her skirt. When she speaks, her voice is hard. "You know I appreciate your family trying to help, and it would have been fun to see your country. But I wouldn't have been happy. I never wanted to be that far from my family. I love it here. This is my life."

"But it doesn't have to be!" I shout. "Who gets married at fourteen?"

"Shhhhh! What's the point of coming all the way down here if you're going to shout to the hilltops? And I'm not getting married at fourteen. I'll be fifteen by the time we get married. Legal age."

I kick a stone and send it sailing across the river. It lands with a plop. I feel like I've been dropped into a National Geographic documentary on underage marriage. We studied it in Social Studies this year, as part of a unit on children's rights. The United Nations wrote a big long document about kids having the right to education, health care, food, shelter and all sorts of stuff. Anyone under eigh-teen is considered a child, according to the UN, and kids aren't supposed to get married.

"You don't understand," Aracely says.

"Uh, yeah. No kidding." I keep kicking stones. She wades back across the river, pulls a plastic bag from her waistband and stoops to yank at a patch of berro.

I stomp across to where she is and snatch handfuls of the little plant from the water. "I can't believe your father agreed to this."

"What's he supposed to do?" She's the one who's shouting now. "Who else is going to marry me looking this way?"

I stare at her. Part of me can't believe she's serious, but the bigger part of me, the part that's known her most of my life, that has watched her try to hide her scar in a million ways, knows she means what she says. I make my voice gentle. "You're more than your scar, Aracely. Anyone who meets you can see that."

She looks up at me, tears in her eyes, tiny berro leaves and their little roots dangling from her hands. "But not everyone's willing to look at *this* for the rest of their lives. Vin doesn't care, and if I marry him, I won't have to leave my family behind. I don't want to be some *gringa* who doesn't belong here anymore, Dian."

I look at her but don't know what to say.

She turns back to the berro, rips out another handful and heads back to the main road.

I follow her and try to get a conversation going again, but it doesn't work. She answers with stiff politeness, like we've only just met, and I know she's waiting for me to take back everything I said against the marriage.

I'm not going to though. I'll never forgive myself if I don't find a way to stop the wedding. I only hope I can do it without losing my best friend.

Three

I should be exhausted. I woke up at dawn, rode in the back of a pickup truck over bumpy roads for three hours to get to Cucubano, hiked down to the river and back with Aracely and stayed up late talking to people from all over the village. My eyes should have closed the instant my head hit the pillow. But hours after I turn out the light, I'm still staring up into the darkness.

The darkness is different here. It's absolute. Nothing distracts me from the terrible images flying around in my head. Aracely at twenty, with a baby on one hip and a toddler clinging to her leg. At twenty-five, skinny, with bags under her eyes and three more kids. By Mom's age, forty-three, she'll be a grandmother. And what if this Vin guy cheats on her? Lots of men here do. Will Aracely put up with that too, because she's afraid to be alone?

I must fall asleep at some point, though, because the next thing I know, a rooster's crowing. It takes me a few seconds to figure out where I am. I bat away the mosquito netting, tiptoe past my snoring parents and let myself into the medical clinic-classroom next door.

The bicycles are behind a stack of boxes. Bike thieves in Canada would turn up their noses at these old clunkers. Half the paint's chipped off them, their handlegrips are held on with brightly colored electrical tape, and they're heavier than any bicycles I've ever lifted.

But riding them is still faster than running, which is why they're here. Every year, the priest in Ocoa lends us two beat-up mountain bikes so my parents can get around in medical emergencies. They've used the bikes a few times: once when María Castillo was in labor, and once when Dad needed to pick up more medical supplies and was about to miss the only bus into the city—two hours away. Mostly, though, the bikes sit at the back of the clinic, collecting orange dust.

My parents don't want me riding them. They say it would set me apart as a rich North American because no one else has a bicycle. This year, though, they're letting me work on them, at least, hidden away behind the clinic where I won't attract attention. I brought all my tools from home, and a friend of the priest sold us some parts before we came to the mountains.

I poke my head out the door and look both ways. The sun's barely up, and for once, no one's around. I push the green bike around the side of the building, and as usual I can smell the outhouses before I even round the corner. Everything else about the spot behind the clinic is perfect. It's private—just two outhouses and a patch of ground fenced in by hundreds and hundreds of Rafael's coffee trees. The sounds of Rafael's pigs and donkey will drown out any noise I make. The stench I could do without, but I'm willing to live with it.

I lean the bicycle against the wall of the clinic. The chain needs greasing. The tires need air. The brakes need tightening. Beyond that, I'm hoping I can find—or at least invent—some deep mechanical problem that'll keep me going all summer.

I need to do something that takes my mind off Aracely, something familiar that reminds me of home. Working on bikes is what I'd be doing in Canada if my parents hadn't insisted on bringing me to another country to wear someone else's old clothes and live the life they want me to lead.

I told them I didn't want to come. Months before they booked our flights, Grandma said I could stay with her if I wanted, and she even gave me tips on how to convince my parents. "You've got to put things in their terms," she said. "Use language they'll understand." I borrowed their favorite parenting book, *Raising a Confident Teenager*, and stole a few key phrases. Then I wrote my speech, memorized it and practiced in front of the mirror. By the time I sat down with my parents at our February family meeting, I thought I stood a good chance of convincing them.

"My time in Cucubano has taught me a lot," I said, my hands clasped under the kitchen table. Every-thing was riding on this one conversation. "I feel it's time for the next step in my personal growth. The bike shop says I can volunteer four times a week this summer if I want to. They'll pay me in bike parts. I'll be doing something I'm passionate about, we can donate the cost of my plane fare to a new well for Cucubano, and our family's carbon footprint will be way smaller this year." Under the table, I crossed my fingers that this would work.

Mom took off her glasses and rubbed her eyes, like this was all too much for her. She looked especially tired that night. She spends her time in Canada working at a medical clinic and being part of seven different environmental organizations. She's always home for family meeting, though, no matter what else is going on in her life. She takes notes that she posts on the fridge afterward, and we all pretend we can read her handwriting. Sometimes I wish I could tell her to just skip our meeting, take a hot bath and go to bed early. I really think it would do her good. I don't think she wants to hear that though.

As Mom massaged her temples, Dad chewed his lip. He was still wearing his spandex shorts from the bike ride home from work, and his salt-and-pepper hair was wavy from being crammed into his helmet. "Dian, thanks for sharing how you feel—"

I winced. *Acknowledge how they feel before telling them what to do.* That's chapter three in the parenting book, and it's never a good sign for the kid.

"I want you to know," Dad continued, "how important it is to us that you come along this summer."

Make her feel valued. Chapter two.

Mom pushed her notepad to the center of the table and leaned toward me. "This is a family project, and you're coming, Dian. That's just the way it is."

Establish authority. Be firm. Mom was headed straight to the end of the book, and if I didn't say something soon, the discussion would be over.

"How is it a family project?" I tried to sound conversational, curious and, above all, *not* confrontational. "Sure, I see you more because you work right next to where we live, but you work most of the time. And I'm with Aracely's family, and whenever we're in the same room, you're talking about patients and I'm pretending not to hear because it's confidential." That part's not much different from life at home in Canada, actually, except that in Cucubano we're all living on top of each other for two months straight. I go from relative freedom here, spending most of my time at Grandma's house and occasionally clashing with my parents when they're home for family meetings, to practically living in their pockets. I don't even have my own room there.

My mother pushed away from the table and opened a cupboard. "I don't know what's gotten into you, Dian. You've been so argumentative since you quit your clubs."

I groaned. It always came back to this. A month earlier, I'd quit the four environmental and social-justice clubs I'd been part of since I was seven. I was sick of talking to the same people about the same stuff all the time. It was bad enough that my parents were always writing letters to the editor about everything from Canadian mining regulations to my school not using recycled paper. Add to that my lack of cell phone, new clothes and family vehicle—as well as my campaigns for the same causes that my parents ranted about—and it was no wonder that kids at school said I'd grow up to be just as much of a wack-job as my parents.

I quit the clubs because I want a life. I don't have to spend every spare moment saving the world. Instead, I spend my time fixing bikes. I love finding exactly what's wrong, making a few changes and having the whole bike working again in just a few hours.

Bikes are simple and fixable. Unlike the rest of the world. I've tried to explain this to my parents. I've pointed out that I'm still doing something sustainable, but I might as well be building SUVs or pesticide sprayers or submachine guns for all the difference it makes to them. Whenever we argue, it comes back to the clubs.

"I'm not more argumentative," I said. "I'm just more sure of what I want. I want to work at the bike shop. I'm happy here. In Cucubano, I don't fit in, and I never will."

"Don't you know how lucky you are to travel?" Mom asked, slathering jam on bread. "How many people would jump at the chance to spend a summer in the Dominican?"

I laughed. "You make it sound like we're going for palm trees, beaches and endless buffets. That's not Cucubano. No one could call *that* a hot-spot destination."

She frowned at me, bit into her sandwich and gazed out the window, like her mind was moving on to other things.

Dad grabbed the pen Mom had left on the table and rolled it around in his fingers. "The teenage years are crucial, Dian. We've talked about this.

The most important thing now is to spend quality family time together, and that's what we're going to do this summer."

"Why do I have to go to the Dominican Republic for that? I'm here all year round, and we never spend time together. What makes you think we suddenly will if we change location?" I was on my feet now. "And what's the point of family meetings if no one wants to hear anything I have to say? Are you done telling me how my life is going to be? Can I go now?"

Dad gave me a pleading look, the kind that means he's doing his best and I'm just not cooperating. Mom snapped out of her window gazing and blinked at me. "I know this is tough for you, Dian. It's tough being a teenager."

Thanks. Thanks a lot.

"We appreciate you coming," Dad said.

"I know, you said that already." I grabbed a jacket and headed for the door.

I didn't speak to them for the next three days. (It took them awhile to notice, because they were hardly home.) Eventually they decided I could work on the emergency bikes while I was in the Dominican. If they expected me to be overjoyed, they were disappointed, but I did start talking to them again, mostly to continue my campaign against coming here.

I reasoned. I yelled. I screamed. I slammed doors. I even considered doing something to get arrested, but everything I thought up seemed rather stupid, and in the end I decided that even Cucubano was better than a juvenile detention center.

That was before my only friend here stopped talking to me.

One of the worst things about Cucubano is how much time I've got to think about stuff, like Aracely getting married. So far, I've come up with exactly zero ways to stop this marriage.

The very worst thing about Cucubano is that from here I can't talk to Grandma or my friend Emily or anyone else who might understand.

The only people I can talk to are my parents.

Four

"You're kidding," Dad says. His Spanish is perfect but heavily accented. It makes me cringe to hear it, but my parents refuse to speak English—or let me speak it—while we're in the Dominican Republic. Dad shakes his head. "She's getting married? Just like that?"

"Not right away," I say. "Next year. Legal age is fifteen with her parents' consent."

Dad looks as stunned as I feel, but my mother is picking at her food, silent. I stare at her. I've seen her fly into a rage about toilet paper being made from trees, but she says nothing about Aracely throwing her future away?

We're sitting around the teacher's desk in our classroom-bedroom at dinnertime on our second day in Cucubano, eating rice and beans. If we drop so much as a grain, we'll attract cockroaches, which are as big as a flash drive in this country, but we'd still rather eat indoors than outside, where Rafael's chickens come to eat off our plates.

"What about Canada?" Dad asks. "She was excited about that idea last year."

I shrug. "She'd rather get married. She wants to stay close to her family."

Mom sighs and looks at me like I'm a hurt toddler she can cure with a hug. "I'm sorry, Di. This must be a shock for you."

Only for me? "She's fourteen, Mom! The guy's nineteen, and she could have five kids by the time she's twenty. You'd have a fit if I were getting married next year to a guy old enough to be in university."

"You're not getting married." She's in Patient Parent Mode, speaking slowly. "And of course he's older. Another fourteen-year-old couldn't support her. Women—girls—marry young here, Dian. You know that."

"It's economic," Dad says.

Mom glares at him. "It's not economic, Todd. It's cultural. You don't see people marrying off their fifteen-year-old sons to the first person who asks."

Dad raises his hands like she's turned a gun on him. "It's not my fault, you know. I did try to help."

Mom purses her lips. "No matter what the cause, it's not our place to try to change this one."

I blink at her. "You're just going to let her get married? After years of ranting about women's rights, you're just going to shrug and let this happen?"

"Who are we to tell them their culture is wrong?" Mom asks, as if she could never imagine going against tradition.

"But it is! Even the United Nations says so. We read about it at school. The UN Convention on the Rights of the Child says no one should get married this young." I can't believe I have to explain this to my parents, of all people. Where do they get off suddenly picking and choosing which human rights they believe in?

"United Nations," Mom says, "is working to change the situation on a large scale, not to break up engagements one at a time. It sounds like Aracely doesn't want us to interfere, Dian."

"Since when has that kind of thing stopped you?" I shout. "This is Aracely we're talking about!"

Dad shoots me a look that means the whole of Cucubano can hear me and I'd better watch my mouth. I clench my teeth and stab my spoon into my rice, but I refuse to stay quiet. How could anyone stay quiet about this?

"She had a way out," I hiss, barely above a whisper. "You offered her one, but now you're just as happy to let her become another baby machine, like all the other women in this village."

"How dare you, Dian Grace?" Mom's the one shouting now, and for once, she switches to English. "How dare you judge the people here like that, talking about them as if they're no more than animals? Just because you don't want what Aracely wants doesn't make her wrong."

"So if she wanted to jump off a bridge, you wouldn't have a problem with that either?" I push my food away. "Don't you get it? She's only doing this because going to Canada terrifies her. She's never even been to a city before, never mind a completely different country. Of course she's scared. But that's no excuse to throw her life away."

Dad looks pained. Bringing her to Canada was his idea, after all. "She told you she's scared?"

I look away. "Not exactly, but I know her well enough."

Mom takes a few deep breaths and returns to Spanish to ask if I'm sure. "*Estás segura*? Maybe you have different definitions of what's important. Do you really know what her life would be like if she left Cucubano behind? Once she goes away and gets an education, she won't be coming back, Dian—not as the same person anyway. The minute she leaves here, she leaves for good, and no one can guarantee her that leaving will make her happier."

For a moment, I hesitate, imagining how Aracely might see Cucubano after living in Canada. I bet she'd think of it as smaller than before, with less to do, with fewer opportunities…

No. I'm not going to think about that. Mom's twisting everything, and I know why she's doing it too. "No matter what I want, you go for the opposite, don't you?" I shout. "If I say I'm against the marriage, then you're all for it."

I jump to my feet and head for the door, but when I get there, I stop. Might as well give them one more thing to chew on before I go. "Did I mention that Vin's working for the mine you've been protesting against for the past two years?"

Dad winces, Mom closes her eyes again, and I know I've hit my mark. I'm sure Vin's mine is the one owned by a Canadian company. My parents have written letters, held marches and organized petitions against it for ages because it pours toxic waste into the rivers, which poisons the people who live nearby. I was tempted to mention all this to Aracely, but what would I say? *Don't marry a guy who works at a mine my parents don't like*? I would sound like some sort of political puppet, and that's exactly the person I'm trying *not* to be.

No reason to hide the mine from my parents though. If they want me to stop caring about Aracely's right to a decent future, then they'll have to stop caring about the mine they've fought against for years. Satisfied, I yank open the door to step outside, but then Dad turns to Mom. "Maybe it's a good sign. Maybe that means people who live close to the mine are refusing to work there. They have to import workers from a few hours away now."

His reaction is so weird that it takes me a few seconds to realize he's missing the point entirely.

"We're not talking about the mine, Dad. We're talking about my friend's *life*."

"You were the one who brought it up," Mom snaps. "And I'll ask you to change your tone when you're talking to us."

"You guys are hopeless." I slam out, not caring if the whole of Cucubano is talking about my bad behavior tomorrow.

I want to tear off down the hill. If I were at home, I would. I'd run until I was exhausted, and then I'd let myself into Grandma's backyard, climb her apple tree and just hang out there until I felt like going home. Sometimes, Grandma sees me up there and pretends not to, unless I wave. If I wave, she comes out to talk, but otherwise she lets me be. She calls my parents to tell them I'm okay, but she doesn't let them come over. She says everyone needs a quiet thinking place, and the apple tree's mine.

Here in Cucubano, I don't have anywhere to go. Sure, there are tons of trees, but getting to them means wandering along the road, and I don't have the guts for that. The settlement is safe enough by day—everyone knows me, I can never go anywhere without three or four children coming along, and being invited here by the priest means that people are extra careful around me and my parents—but nighttime is different. No one is out at night unless they're coming back from the *colmado*, drunk. And there's no telling what drunken guys might do if it's too dark for anyone to see them.

I sit behind the school, rest my head on my knees and cover my ears, but I can still hear my parents debating whether to run after me and demand more respect. I jab my fingers in my ears and hum.

I don't go back in until the lights are out. My parents pretend to be asleep, but I know they're not because they're not snoring like they always do. They're still quiet when *I* finally fall asleep.

❧

"What you said isn't true, you know," Dad says over breakfast the next morning. It's Canada Day, and if we were back home, we'd be celebrating all things Canadian, including laws against fifteen-year-olds getting married. Instead, we're here in the Dominican Republic, and my parents are still trying to convince me that it's perfectly reason-able for Aracely to throw her life away. "We haven't given up on her," Dad's saying. "I think we have to respect her decision."

"How can you respect a decision made for all the wrong reasons?" As soon as the words fly out of my mouth, I want to bite them back. They're my parents' words, and they use them for just about everything they believe in: if everyone knew all the facts about global warming, no one would drive cars anymore, et cetera, et cetera. They figure it's our family's mission to educate people to make the "right" decisions.

If Mom recognizes the words, she doesn't say anything. She bites down hard on her toast instead.

"Just keep talking to Aracely," Dad says. "Find out more before you pass judgment."

How am I supposed to find out more when we're barely on speaking terms?

We eat the rest of our breakfast in silence, and we're cleaning up when Mom announces how I'm going to spend my day. Apparently, I'll be doing all the chores that Aracely's mom used to do for us. "The veggie patch needs serious weeding, and we need more washing powder from the colmado. Get some more bread too, while you're at it, please.

After lunch, I want you to run down to María's place to drop off a cream I promised her yesterday."

I don't know whether these chores are necessities or punishment or both. Mom doesn't say, although she does raise her eyebrows at me like she's waiting for me to protest. But why would I bother? I'm not going to pretend to spend the day with Aracely's mom like my parents assume I usually do. And I'm relieved to have something to do. Any of the neighbors' kids that I see on the road will come with me, distracting me with their chatter. It's better than sitting around here, wishing I were anywhere else.

Or worrying about Aracely, which I've been doing pretty much every spare moment. When she's old, will she think back to this summer as the moment when everything changed? Will she imagine herself dividing in two, one that married and one that didn't? And will her married self miss the person she could have been?

The images in my head have gotten worse. Now when I picture her at age twenty-five, she glares back at me, like I should have done something to save her.

Five

Clouds roll in, and rain pours down like it'll never stop. Most of Cucubano goes to sleep because the aguacero on metal roofs is the only thing that drowns out Rafael's donkey, pigs and roosters.

In summer—rainy season—the weather and its patterns are always the same. The morning is sunny and warm. We finish lunch, the skies open, it pours, we go to sleep, and we wake up a few hours later when the sky is blue again and the sun has baked the muddied road hard. Today my mother wakes me up from my *siesta*. She stands by my bed, holding out a tube of cream that I'm supposed to take to María. Mom's smiling, but only barely.

I know she's still mad about my baby-machine comment, and she'll only get madder if I try to explain. I don't think girls are stupid for staying here and having lots of kids. I just hate that it feels like the only option.

"I wrote the instructions on this piece of paper," Mom says. "Read them to María."

I squint at her scrawly writing the way I always do. "I'll try."

Mom laughs and folds her arms across her chest, but we're both smiling a bit more now.

Mom's eyes scan mine, and she hesitates before she speaks. "We're not trying to go against everything you think, Dian. We're honestly not sure that stepping in would be the right thing to do here. It's nothing against you, you know."

Part of me wants that pitying hug she almost gave me last night, and the rest of me wants to yell at her again. Instead, I mumble something about getting the cream to María and head out the door. Behind me, I imagine the hurt expression on Mom's face, but what does she expect? Would it really kill her to consider my opinion for once?

I'm usually still napping at this time. The road is solid but springy under my feet. A few meters downhill, two little kids in jeans and T-shirts are slapping the only surviving mud puddle with sticks. They shriek each time one of them gets splashed, and they remind me of my first summer here. I was fascinated by the rain and the muddy road, and I dragged Aracely out for walks as soon as the rain stopped, before the earth had even dried. We marched all over Cucubano, adding an inch of orange mud to the bottoms of our feet with each step. We always came home half a head taller, orange mud spattered to our knees and grinning.

I smile and wave at the kids. They charge over and hug me—big, full-bodied hugs that hold nothing back—and they tell me they're going to stay up late tonight to look for *cucuyos*. I wish I were seven again and could race along with them, trapping fireflies. I picture careful fingers slipping the lid onto a jar, beautiful light dancing inside. Another Aracely memory threatens to flood my brain, but I push it back and grab the outstretched hands of the two nearest kids, and together we head down the hill.

When I round the corner where Aracely lives, I pretend not to see her house, and if the kids notice how hard I'm pretending, they don't say anything. Aracely's house is like most others in Cucubano: a one-room wooden hut with a roof made of thick grass. Most of the building is painted peach, but a few boards have no paint at all. Around the outside, orange and yellow flowers grow as high as my waist.

The door is closed, and the house has no windows. I wonder if Aracely's in there, or if she's out collecting herbs with her abuela. Maybe she's gone to visit a relative. (Or the house of the people who will soon be her relatives. Ugh.) And I wonder if she misses me, or if she's still too angry. Maybe she barely notices that we're not spending time together. She's used to living here without me, after all. For the first time, I wonder if it bothers her that I go away all the time, leaving her behind to live her same old life.

But she says she's happy here. The memory of Mom's voice invades my thoughts. Her twisted arguments have messed with my thinking. If I keep listening to her and Dad, I'll be helping out at the wedding feast, throwing flowers and shouting encouragement, or whatever people do at weddings here.

I've got to get Aracely back, the old Aracely who sat on the floor of our hideout asking me about Canada. *That* Aracely had the guts to want to travel and run after her dreams. She was ready to come to Canada for high school and university, and she was excited about all the stuff we would do together. I'd said I would teach her to ride a bicycle, and we'd work on her English together, and we'd go to school dances and blow people away with our moves. I'd have a sister for the first time in my life.

But maybe I had freaked her out. Maybe I'd described a world so different that she felt like she'd be moving to Jupiter. New language. New customs. New food. She'd have to learn how to take a bus, and how to get to places according to street signs instead of landmarks that she'd seen every day for her entire life. She'd have to choose food at supermarkets hundreds of times bigger than the colmado here, with twenty varieties of milk, dozens of kinds of bread and all sorts of stuff that she'd never seen before. She'd go from knowing everyone to knowing hardly anyone, and she'd go for weeks, maybe months, without news from her family.

Of course she was terrified. I shouldn't have told her so much, but it was too late now to take it back.

The kids and I are halfway to María's house when someone comes pelting around the corner toward us. He's a few years older than me, and he's running like someone's life depends on it.

"Your papá there?" he shouts as he passes.

It's Nerick, who lives in the shack at the bottom of the hill. He looks desperate. Someone in his family needs a doctor. Fast.

"*Sí*," I call back. "Both my parents are there." I don't ask what happened. This is no time to chat, and news will be all over the village within hours anyway.

We don't get many medical emergencies. People are so used to living without a doctor that it takes a lot for them to come running for one. When María Castillo almost died giving birth that time, it took hours for her to agree to let my mother come see her. I wish I knew what's happened in Nerick's family, and I wish I could help.

But instead I stand there watching him race up the hill and cross my fingers that everything will be all right.

Nerick and I used to be friends. Not as close as Aracely and I, but on days when Aracely couldn't play, he seemed to show up out of nowhere. He showed me his favorite spots—the beet field on the hill where we could see the entire valley, the meadow behind the coffee warehouse where the grass was tall enough for us to hide in, the tops of the tallest trees along the road. He always won the race up to those treetops, but he never rubbed it in, just flashed me a grin and joked about throwing things at people down below. He never seemed to care that I was a girl. And I never really cared that all the other kids—except for Aracely—didn't like him much. I noticed it and didn't understand it, but didn't care.

I was seven when I overheard adults warning my parents not to let me play with the Haitian kid. (Nerick was born here, but his parents are from the country next door. They're black and so is he, so everyone calls him Haitian, even though he's never even been to Haiti.) He might put spells on me, they said. My parents said that was nonsense and told me to keep on playing with Nerick for as long as I wanted to. So I did, right up until two years ago, when he stopped showing up at the clinic.

It turned out Nerick's father had taken off, and that meant Nerick had to work, doing odd jobs for anyone who would hire a twelve-year-old. I should have gone to visit, to say hello, at least, when he didn't come around anymore, but what could I say to someone who'd lost his dad and had had to quit school to help feed the family? I said nothing, and now it's been years since we've talked. I hate that he's sprinting up the hill to get medical help and I'm just standing here, wondering what to do.

I turn and walk quickly down the hill to María's. I'm not going to make the same mistake with Aracely that I did with Nerick. I'm not going to pretend nothing's happening. I won't stay quiet until it's too late. I'll find a way to change Aracely's future, and next year, when I've convinced my parents to let me stay in Canada, I'll think back to this summer and know I did the right thing.

❧

Dad's away with Nerick for a long time, and Mom and I are sitting down to supper when he pedals home. His pant legs are covered in orange dust up to the knees, and his shirt is drenched with sweat and is sticking to him. "I guess you can't make either of those old clunkers any easier to ride, can you?" he asks after he puts the bike away.

I shake my head and ask what happened.

"His brother Wilkens was clearing land. The machete went through his foot, he lost a lot of blood, and he passed out. I think it was more shock than blood loss that made him pass out though. I've got him on antibiotics, and I hope I've scared him into resting for the next few days. I'll go back tomorrow to check in."

I nod. Things like this happen a lot here. Usually my parents hear about it long afterward, when the gash is infected because people can't afford to stop working in the fields. I'm glad Nerick came for help, and I hope his brother gets better soon. At moments like this, I feel like a spoiled brat for ever complaining about anything.

Six

"I want to learn how to do that." Nerick is wearing tight jeans and a white T-shirt without a streak of orange earth on it anywhere. Since I saw him yesterday, he's lost that terrified look. He's looking down at me, his hands in his pockets, like a model in one of the teen magazines I see at the library.

My hands are covered in bike grease. Some of it's probably smudged across my cheek. My hair is in a messy ponytail, and my outfit is one of the worst in the whole donation pile (a shirt with yellow stripes and little orange smiley-faces, and baggy, bright red shorts). And, of course, I'm squatting between a bicycle and an outhouse, fiddling with a derailleur, surrounded by stench. "Learn what?" I ask.

"What you're doing." His eyes meet mine but then dart away. "Your dad says you know how to fix bikes, and I want to learn."

I blink at him, not sure what's most stunning: that my father—Dr. "Keep the Bikes Hidden or Woe to You"—has told Nerick I'm working on them; that a teenage guy wants me to teach him to fix bikes; or that Nerick wants to learn to fix something he's probably never ridden before. The emergency bike might be the only one he's ever seen.

I feel my face pull into a smile. Ever since I started work at the bike shop back home, my friend Emily has worried about my romantic future. She's even suggested I wear rubber gloves to prevent blackening of nail beds and cuticles, and now I get to tell her that the hottest guy in Cucubano wants to spend time with me because I'm a grease monkey.

He frowns and crosses his arms. "Look, if you don't want to teach me, that's—"

"No, no!" I say before he gets the wrong idea. Sometimes I get so lost in my own thoughts that people assume I disagree with them. It happens with Emily all the time, and it drives her crazy. "Sure, I'll teach you."

He grins and crouches down beside me. "Good. I could give you a few pointers on tree climbing in exchange, if you like."

I laugh. I love that he's teasing me again like he used to. "Deal."

He pulls a red handkerchief out of his back pocket and unwraps two small pieces of sugarcane. "Want some? It fell off one of the trucks going by."

I know this is payment for the bike-repair lessons, and I smile. Sugarcane grows almost everywhere in the country except here. The mountains get too cold for it to grow, so it's a rare treat. He peels back the dark outer skin and hands me a piece. I suck on it, pulling the sweet juice into my mouth, and thank him.

"*De nada*." He waves a hand at the bike. "Go back to what you were doing."

I show him the derailleur and how it helps move the chain to different gears. I explain how the gears make it easier or harder to pedal the bike. He nods and chews on his lip, concentrating as if I might quiz him on this later. I wonder if any of this makes sense to someone who's never ridden a bike before, but there's no point asking because I can't offer to let him ride anyway. My parents would flip. They might even flip about him being back here with me, learning this. Right now, they're in the clinic. The back window is closed, and with all the chatter at the front of the clinic, I doubt they can hear us. What they don't know won't hurt them.

I finish explaining how the bike works. Nerick nods slowly and smiles.

"So why do you want to learn?" I ask.

"A guy came by the house a few months ago," Nerick says. "He was riding a bicycle that had bags hanging off the front and the back, and he asked if he could pitch a tent near our place. He ate with us and left us a bit of money, and he said he wants to build a big house near here for travelers who are riding their bicycles through the mountains. He'll need all kinds of workers for his business, including bike mechanics. Last night, your papá said you know about fixing bikes. If you teach me, I can be ready when the man shows up again."

I try to look happy for him, but I'm already hoping he doesn't get hurt. I'd hate for Nerick to spend his whole summer learning bike mechanics and dreaming of this guy coming back, only to be disappointed.

At first, I'm surprised that no one else has mentioned this bicycle tourist. Then again, no one talks to Nerick's family much. Their house is at the bottom of the hill, and the only reason they have to come up here is for the medical clinic. Even then, people don't treat them the way they treat my family and other families in the village. When they look at Nerick, all they see is the color of his skin, and that's enough to stop them from having anything to do with him.

"Are you going to the market on Saturday?" he asks, and I yank myself out of my thoughts.

"I don't know. Why?"

The market is in the next town over, about an hour's walk away. People go there to sell their vegetables and to buy things they can't get at the colmado. My parents usually pay Aracely's mom to go for them if they need anything. I've been a few times with Aracely's family but not often. I don't know why Nerick thinks I would go now.

"I thought Aracely might have asked you," he says, "to help her with the herbs."

I swallow, wishing I knew what he was talking about. Aracely's been learning about herbs from her abuela for as long as I can remember, but I don't know what that has to do with the market. Her abuela has always insisted that healing herbs can't be bought and sold. It goes against some kind of basic philosophy about the right to health or something.

"Her bag on the way there is getting bigger and bigger, and it always comes back close to empty." Nerick frowns. "You didn't know about this? She didn't tell you?"

I feel my face going hot. "It never came up." The only thing she told me about was the marriage, and as soon as I said what I thought of *that*, she stopped talking to me. But this market thing could be my in. "I might go with Aracely on Saturday. I'll ask her later if she wants help."

"I'll see you there then. Or tomorrow, if you're working on the bike again."

"I'll be here." I wave a hand at the outhouses and the crummy old bike. "Come whenever you want."

I know I shouldn't be so available. Emily, who never even speaks to guys she likes, would be appalled. And even Aracely says to be careful about showing too much interest. But the guy Emily likes doesn't even know she exists, and Aracely is getting married at fifteen, so I'm not going to follow their guy advice. From now on, I'll invent my own. It's not like he's interested in *me* anyway. It's the bikes. So who cares if I look desperate for friendship? Anyone can see it's the truth.

Seven

I'm not desperate enough to talk to Aracely though. In fact, I avoid her. When she comes up the hill with her sister, I dash into the clinic. If I'm on the road and I hear her voice around the curve, I jump onto a trail in the bush. Whichever children are with me think it's a hilarious new game I've invented, and they stay stock-still among the leaves and then burst into giggles the second Aracely's out of earshot. Each time this happens, I'm hiding almost before I notice what I'm doing. I feel like a coward, but I tell myself I need time to think.

Meanwhile, all over the village, people are asking questions. The first few days we were here,

they kept asking where Aracely was and looked
shocked when I said I didn't know. We used to
be inseparable. So I made up some lame excuse
about both of us being busy, and people nodded
and talked about the responsibilities of growing
up, but they still looked suspicious.

Ten days have passed, and the questions are more
blunt. Yesterday, Miralis Vargas asked me if Aracely
and I are fighting. Miralis lives across the road from
us, and Aracely and I call her the Eye because she's
always watching everybody and spreading stories
about everything she sees. I'm sure she didn't
believe my line about both Aracely and me being
very busy, but no way would I tell her anything else.

Even my parents want to know what's going on.
"You're very quiet lately," Mom says at supper one
night. "What's up?"

"Not much." I spend my days running errands
for my parents, working in the garden and teaching
Nerick about bikes whenever he shows up. (One
Saturday has gone by since his first visit, when he
asked if I was going to market. I'm sure he noticed
that I didn't go, but he hasn't brought it up again.
Maybe he knows Aracely and I are fighting, but
he, at least, figures it's none of his business.)

My parents found out right away about Nerick's visits. They said they're happy we're friends again but can't understand why he wants to learn bike mechanics. I haven't told them about the cycling tourist Nerick met. I love the fact that no one in Cucubano knows about this yet, and I don't want to be the one to start the gossip flying.

Mom watches the oregano leaves float around in her soup and says nothing. Since our fight about my friend the day after we got here, no one has mentioned Aracely. My parents give me enough work to keep me busy, and I try not to be around when Aracely's mother comes to deliver our meals. My parents pretend this is all normal and never mention it, in case I start shouting again and make the neighbors talk. (I never expected my family to worry about that kind of thing, since they have no trouble making a spectacle of themselves for a worthy cause at home. But I guess different rules apply when it comes to me making a scene for something *I* care about.)

Mom's voice is hushed, almost a whisper, when she asks about Aracely tonight. "You don't see her much anymore, do you?"

I shake my head and give my standard line, although I know they'll see right through it. "Too busy, I guess."

Mom reaches over and touches my hand. "I'm sorry, Dian." She sounds like she means it. I *could* point out why it's pointless to be sorry when she could actually be doing something to fix the situation, but I'm tired. Tired of thinking about this all the time. Tired of being the only one to fight for Aracely's rights.

"Thanks," I mumble and slurp my soup.

Dad looks between the two of us. Mom sighs, and Dad hesitates before he says, "We're thinking of going up to the *finca* this Saturday morning." I snap from tiredness to self-preservation. I hate the finca, and I feel guilty for hating it. Everyone there does the best they can in their situation, but their situation makes me too sad for words. I've only gone once, when I was about eight, and I've refused to go back since.

The finca is a coffee plantation far off the road. It takes two hours to walk there: up the road that leads to a path through a dozen fields to another road, and then along another path and up another mountain. The views over the valley could sell a million postcards (if anyone was crazy enough to make postcards of Cucubano), and each time we go up that remote road, people stop to talk or to offer us everything from bananas to tomatoes to yams. The first time my family went to the finca, Donal Marte, the owner, showed us how they dry the coffee, pack it into sacks, sew the sacks shut and then haul out the beans on the backs of donkeys. It sounded just like the coffee commercials I'd seen on Grandma's TV, and I couldn't wait to tell her that places like this really exist. I borrowed Dad's camera and took dozens of photos of the yellowed beans and the sacks, and even a few close-ups of the donkey.

Then the owner took us over to the cook-shack, and we met his wife. She gave me a sweet orange, and I was happily munching away on it when Donal led us to another small building. If I'd been listening to what he was saying, I might have been ready for what was inside, but when he pushed the door open, I was shocked. Inside, slumping on chairs in the darkness, were two teenagers, drooling on themselves and smelling of pee.

I started crying, and Mom had to take me out and explain to me that the parents were doing the best they could. These kids had developmental problems, and no one had expected them to survive infancy. They couldn't go to special schools like we have in Canada because that kind of school doesn't exist around here. The best their parents could do was keep them healthy and safe by locking them inside so they couldn't wander off into the bush.

None of that made me feel any better, and I cried all the way home. I still get tears in my eyes when I think about it. How can life be so random that I was born healthy into a Canadian family with money when those teenagers have to spend their whole lives alone in a dark hut?

My parents go see them every year and tend to any health issues the family might have. I always stay with Aracely, and I bet my parents are disappointed in me because they want me to be the kind of person who sees terrible things and helps solve the problem, but that's not me. I can't go back. I won't.

"I'm going to the market this Saturday," I tell my parents now. "Nerick said Aracely usually brings a lot of stuff to sell, and I thought I'd offer to help."

"Well done, Di." Dad claps me on the back. "I knew you'd find a way to work through this stuff. I'm very proud of you."

My face gets hot, and I look away. It's been a long time since he's said that.

Mom is smiling at me. "You're a good kid, you know that?"

I drain the last of my soup and try not to think of the conversation I now have to have with my former friend.

❦

"If you're going to keep ranting at me, I don't want to hear it."

Aracely is in the garden patch behind her house that afternoon. I've told my little friends that I need to talk to her alone, which they thought was weird, but they've gone off to play up the road. Aracely's wearing a tight green skirt and a white blouse. Her hair's pulled back in a neat ponytail at the base of her neck, and she doesn't look at me as she snatches at weeds between the tomato plants. I hate how grown-up she looks, as if she's trying to play the part of the almost-married woman.

I banish that thought and focus on what I have to say. By now, I've replayed our fight so often in my mind that I'm starting to think she has every right to be mad at me. I'm the one who scared her out of coming to Canada, after all. If I hadn't talked so much about all the stuff we'd do together—stuff that was very exciting to me but probably terrifying to her—she might still be planning to come.

It's my job to unscare her, I've decided. To reassure her that she doesn't have to learn everything immediately, that I'll be with her every step of the way. We could even start practicing English together. Before any of that happens, though, we've got to be friends again. "I'm not going to rant," I tell her. "I'm sorry I hurt your feelings." That's true, at least.

She stops weeding and stands to face me. Her eyes are narrowed and her lips are tight, but her eyes meet mine. For a terrible moment, I think she'll demand that I take back everything I said that day by the river, but she dusts off her hands and steps forward to kiss my cheeks. "Thank you for coming, Dian. Would you like something to drink?"

I flinch at her formal tone. Is she doing this because she still doesn't trust me, or is this part of her new soon-to-be-a-married-woman personality?

"I'm fine, thanks," I tell her. "I was wondering if you want help bringing your herbs to the market on Saturday."

She smiles and doesn't bother asking how I know about the herbs since she never got around to telling me. She's used to everyone knowing everyone's business. "Yes, please. It'll be easier with two."

"You usually do it by yourself?"

She nods and bends down to pinch a sucker off a tomato plant. "My parents are too busy, and you know what Abuela is like. She's never accepted money for herbs—just food and whatever people want to give her—and she refuses to help me if money is involved. She doesn't have any problem eating the food that the money buys though." Aracely's face softens into a smile. She could forgive her grandmother anything, I know. In that way, we're a lot alike. Our grandmothers have always had more time for us than our parents have, and we could argue with our grandmothers until we'd run out of breath but still know we'd be completely lost without them.

I ask her what time I should show up, and she says six in the morning. At home, I'd never dream of waking up so early on a Saturday, but here it's normal.

"It'll be fun!" I say in Spanish, and then, heart racing, I say the same thing in English. This is part of my plan, but I don't know how she'll take it. I've never spoken English around her, but if I start now, she'll learn plenty of phrases by the end of the summer. Life in Canada won't seem as scary if she knows some of the language. "I've been thinking I could teach you some English this summer. I mean, you taught me Spanish when we were kids. I'd like to give something back to you."

She laughs. "Thanks, I guess, but what on earth am I going to use English for?" Her eyes fix on mine. I swallow hard, and she must see my nervousness, because the smile slides off her face. "What am I going to need English for, Dian?"

My face burns.

"You don't give up, do you?" Her voice is like a slap. "You come here to apologize, but then you go right back to pushing for what you want. You're still trying to convince me to go to your country, aren't you?"

I take a step back. Onto a tomato plant. I jump forward and scuttle out of Aracely's way. "I just thought it might be useful—"

"Useful if I go to Canada, but not here, Dian." She bats a wisp of her hair out of her face. "Why don't you get that I'm happy here? Why is it so hard to understand that I want to keep living right here, not in some foreign place where I'll never fit in? Just because you travel in airplanes and live in a big house and own your own bicycle doesn't give you the right to tell me how to live my life." She waves a hand at the scar across her cheek. "This is me, and this is what I want. You have no right to tell me it's wrong."

She pushes past me into the house. I know better than to follow.

Eight

I spend the next day feeling like someone stuck my brain in a washing machine. My thoughts are spinning too fast to make any sense. Most of the time, I know Aracely's being totally unfair, but then a sharp question pelts me out of nowhere: Is there any part of me that's as stuck-up as she says?

Nerick hasn't come today, so I'm caught in this spin cycle right up until suppertime, when my parents yank my attention in another direction.

"We'd like you to move the bike lessons," Dad says as he ladles out the soup. "Patients can hear you and Nerick talking through the window."

I look up from my bowl. "Does that matter? They can probably hear everyone who's talking on the front steps too."

"Yes, but they've walked past those people already. They know they're there. They don't expect people to be listening in from the outhouses."

"We're not listening in!" I say. "If you ever took two seconds to watch us out there, you'd know that Nerick's busy memorizing every adjustment I make. What difference would it make if *I* were listening in anyway? You talk about all your patients at every meal."

My parents give each other those serious looks they don't think I can read. *Oh crap! She's on to us! What do we do now?* They might as well be saying the words out loud.

Dad places his spoon in his bowl and leans his forearms on the desk. "What we talk about is always confidential, Dian. You know that, and we trust you."

"But you don't trust Nerick?"

Mom jumps in to help with the defense. "This isn't a question of us trusting you or him. It's about how the patients feel."

"Bull." I'm tempted to say much worse, but that'll divert the conversation into a parental tirade against swearing, and I want them to listen to what I have to say. I'm calling my parents' bluff. People here talk about everything from their fertility to their bowel functions. Bodies and how they work—or don't—are just part of life. And they'll talk about that stuff to anyone. Or almost anyone. "It's the whole Haitian thing again, isn't it?" I ask. "If it were any other kid back there, no one would care, but they don't want Nerick and his family around."

Dad sighs. "I wish people were different, but this is another big cultural issue that we can't change. Please just help us out on this one, and find somewhere else to work on the bikes."

"Help you out?" I ask. "Help you out? Like coming here isn't enough? Like working in your garden and running your errands doesn't cut it? Now you want me to give up the one thing I like doing? Because you've got a bunch of racist patients?"

"Who said anything about giving up the bikes?" Mom asks.

"You did!" I'm shouting now. It's only the second week of July. What am I going to do the rest of the summer without the bikes? "You know the back is the only place we can work on them without being seen. So if you don't want us back there, and you don't want people to see us, you don't want me working on the bikes!"

"Please calm down." Dad looks pained.

"You're afraid the neighbors will hear, aren't you?" I ask. "Why are you so worried about what the neighbors think all of a sudden? Couldn't you care about that when we're home, when it would actually be useful?"

I dump my cup and spoon into my empty bowl and slam out of the room.

❧

That night I dream about the hideout, and I'm still thinking about it when I wake up. I wonder what it's like now, covered with vines again. How much do vines grow in a year? And could I clear them myself and use the house just for me? Could I ever get a bike there, and what would Aracely say if she found out I was sharing our secret spot with Nerick?

I shake the thoughts out of my head. Someone would see me bringing the bike there, for sure.

And they'd definitely see Nerick going onto Aracely's uncle's land, which would cause problems. I'd still like to go back there myself, though, to see what it's like. I could use a dose of privacy right now.

I watch my parents roll out of bed before sunrise. It takes me a few seconds to figure out why they're up so early. It's Saturday. They're going to the finca. I'm supposed to be going to the market. I haven't told my parents that Aracely and I fought again.

I get up and pretend I need to be at Aracely's place by six. My parents and I are silent at breakfast, and when they wish me a good day at the market, I thank them and give nothing away. They'd be horrified at the thought of me on my own all day. When I'm running errands, they at least know where I am at any given moment. They're convinced that if I don't have a set schedule of things to do, I'll wind up walking off a cliff or getting poisoned in a cloud of pesticide as someone sprays tomato crops. No, my parents would postpone their day trip for sure if they knew I wasn't going to the market. No way am I going to risk the luxury of an entire day to myself.

The second they disappear over the hill, I throw some things in a bag and hop over the fence into the coffee trees of Rafael's *cafetál*. The best way to get to the hideout is from a trail up the road, but that would mean walking right past the Eye, and I don't want people talking.

The coffee trees are dense beneath the taller trees, and every few meters a banana tree nestles up to the narrow path between the plants. The sun filters down in dancing wisps, and the only sound is the breeze among the leaves and my flip-flops clapping against the ground. It feels weird to be alone—it hardly ever happens here, and no one on earth has any idea where I'm going—but it feels good too. Aracely and I came through here a million times last summer, and I'll be careful.

I follow the trail down a slope, and when the coffee trees end, I'm in José's beet field. On the other side is a big rock that Aracely and I used to climb to see the entire valley down below. If the wind picked up and we spread our arms wide, we felt like we could fly.

Down the hill, almost hanging on the edge of a cliff, is an orange house where Aracely's cousin Julia lives. She's nineteen, and from here I can see her two little kids playing in front of the house. Her husband is probably working, and I know that if she sees me, she'll invite me in. I hurry across the field without looking up. The last person I want to see right now is Aracely's favorite cousin, who adores her kids and is probably thrilled that she got married at fifteen.

If anyone has spotted me, I don't notice. I duck into the shade of the banana trees at the end of the field before anyone can call my name. The trees are tall again here, and the underbrush is thick, but the trail to the hideout is much more obvious than I'd expected. When Aracely and I came here for the first time last summer, we spent an entire afternoon just whacking out a trail. No need to do that this time. Someone's been here very recently.

Aracely would have mentioned someone having taken over the house again, wouldn't she? I know it's supposed to belong to her youngest uncle now, but he lives with her family because he never got married.

Whoever's living there, I'm sure they won't mind a visit, I reason. People here never seem to, which is something I love. The times I've dropped in on friends in Canada, people come to the door and stare at me like they don't understand why I'm there, and after a few minutes of conversation, they disappear inside their houses again. Here, people pull out their best plates and put together a big snack and something to drink. It doesn't matter how busy they are, they always seem to have time for visitors.

The house looks exactly as it did when I left it last summer. The door is shut, but not a vine or plant is climbing any part of the wall or the grass roof.

"*Hola*," I call with a loud clap. I don't expect an answer, because if the door is closed, it's unlikey anyone's inside. Electricity doesn't reach this far, and the house has no windows. I knock on one wall, call again and push open the door.

The dirt floor is swept clean. A small home-made altar stands in one corner, and a little table in the opposite corner is the only furniture. Rows and rows of drying plants hang upside down from the ceiling. Herbs. Herbs that will probably be going to market next Saturday. Why didn't she say anything?

It's still there, but I'd rather go to the river, Aracely said when I asked her about this place two weeks ago. I assumed she felt guilty for letting vines grow over our hideout, but I guess she just didn't want me here. Why? Did she think I'd be mad at her for using this place for herself? Why would I care? She's the one who lives here all year round.

I step inside. It smells of dust and *ruda*, a stinky plant that people here burn to chase away evil spirits. A fallen leaf crunches under my feet. I can hear birds singing outside, and the wind rustling the vines. I walk across the room to the table. On top is one of the zippable sandwich bags that we bring from Canada every year. Inside it is the notebook Aracely and I started last summer.

Writing in it was more something to do than anything else. We wrote about who we'd be when we grew up. I was going to be an honest politician, and she was going to be a doctor like my mom, except that she'd use traditional herbs, too, like her abuela does. We wrote about the vacations we'd take together with our kids, and how they would speak both English and Spanish and would feel just as at home in Canada as in the Dominican Republic. Aracely had drawn pictures of the fancy clothes we'd wear when we were grown-up and glamorous. She's always been an amazing artist.

I'm better with words, so I'd written lists of the kinds of changes we'd make in the world.

This was all before I decided *not* to grow up to be exactly like my parents, and Aracely decided she *would* be exactly like hers.

I unzip the bag and slide out the notebook. It doesn't have that crackling new feeling anymore. The edges of the page are wiggly, not bookstore flat. I open the first page, but someone's ripped out our stories. In their place, a drawing of Aracely's abuela stares back at me, unsmiling. It's as if Aracely has frozen her in time. Every shadow in her skin is shaded with pencil, and her eyes meet mine—steady, unwavering and waiting for answers, exactly as they do in real life. The next page is Aracely's mother sleeping, her eyes scrunched shut and one arm over her head, like she's blocking out the noise of daily life. On another page, Aracely's sister laughs up at me from the paper, and on the flipside, I recognize the cousin whose house on the hill I just walked past.

I turn the pages and see the meadow in a stream of sunshine, kids laughing as they swim in the river, people dancing at the colmado and fireflies flitting between the hands of children. She's drawn all the things she loves best about Cucubano—the things I love too.

For an instant, I wonder what it feels like to love a place and be so sure about it that you never want to explore any other.

She's afraid, I remind myself. *It's not the same thing.*

I turn another page and see a young man I've only met a few times. The last time I saw him, he was a skinny teenager who wore clothes that were too big for him. In these pictures, though, he's grown into his clothes. He's smiling, and his eyes meet mine, content. It's Vin. Vin dancing in the colmado. Vin talking with Aracely's father. A pair of hands. (Vin's, I'm sure.) Vin. Vin. Vin. He fills at least half the book. He's dark and slender. He wears his hair short, and the corners of his eyes scrunch up when he smiles, which he does a lot, according to the drawings. His hands look strong and work-roughened, and I can imagine Aracely's smaller hands in his.

I know that hand holding probably hasn't happened in real life yet. All dating here is chaperoned, and I'd bet all my bike tools that Aracely

and Vin have never even been alone together.
Emily couldn't believe it when I told her that this
is how things are here.

"But what about the spark?" she asked. "What if
you marry someone, and when he kisses you on
your wedding night, you don't feel any passion
whatsoever?"

I shrugged. "I guess it's just a risk you have to
take."

"Oh my god," she said. "No way would I marry
a guy I'd never even kissed before."

At the time, what she had said made sense. I've
never even kissed a guy, so I don't know anything
about spark. Looking down at Aracely's drawings, though, I can't imagine that they *wouldn't*
have spark. The way she's drawn him, I can see
why she fell in love. I can imagine his soft touch,
his whispers, how he might stroke the hair away
from her face and she would smile up at him.
I flip another page. Vin and Aracely stand smiling
in front of a house. This house. The one I'm
standing in right now.

Maybe *that's* why she didn't tell me. She wanted
it to be a surprise. She wanted to bring me here
later and show me how well she's doing—her

own business, a future husband and, one day, this house. She wanted me to be happy for her, and instead I shouted. I feel a flicker of guilt, and this time when I remind myself that I have to stop this underage marriage, I'm not so sure of myself anymore.

I'm standing in the house where one day they will make babies. And this is where their children will be born, while I'm at home fixing bikes and reading fashion blogs with Emily. I still don't like it, but I'm not so sure that matters anymore.

Nine

Two days later, I'm standing in front of Nerick's house. The roof is metal, the jagged wooden boards of the walls are painted turquoise, the door is wide open, and inside, a girl is sweeping out clouds of orange dust while two kids play behind her. I wave, and three young faces stare at me. The girls are all wearing their hair in two short, stiff braids sticking out from the sides of their heads, a playful hairstyle that doesn't match their serious, unsmiling faces.

"Hola," I call to them. They wave back but still don't smile, like they're not sure what to make of me. I'm used to kids here running up to me to show off the cucuyos they've caught in a jar, or the soccer move they've been practicing with a balled-up newspaper, or the mud pie they've made for their dolls. My little friends accompanied me halfway down the hill and only headed back home when I told them I was visiting Nerick. They'd heard about his brother's injury and assumed my father had sent me, but no way were they going with me to a Haitian's house. Seven years old and already they can't stand people with dark skin. It makes me sad.

And maybe the three little girls frown at me because they're used to people having nothing to do with them. I smile even wider at them, but their shyness makes me feel like an intruder. "Is Nerick home?" I ask.

The oldest girl whispers a barely audible no. I ask if their mother is around. They point to the cookshack a few meters away.

I step between aloe-vera plants and skirt a few pecking chickens. The walk down the hill has turned my feet and flip-flops orange, but the rest of me is presentable for once. I'm tired of Nerick seeing me in polka dots and tie-dye smeared with grease, so today I've chosen khaki shorts and a fluorescent pink blouse. It's totally not my style. (Why doesn't anyone ever donate tight capris and cute tank tops before we come here?) But at least this outfit passes for style of some sort, which is an improvement over everything else I've worn this summer.

The cookshack is made of poles, with potato-sack walls and a grass roof. "Hola!" I call again, and Nerick's mother sticks her head out of the opening.

In the split second before she sees me, her face is slack and tired. She's thin and her hair is pulled back in a hasty ponytail, but once her eyes meet mine, she grins and immediately looks ten years younger. "Dian! *Bienvenida!*" she welcomes me awkwardly in Spanish. She's lived here longer than I've been alive, but she speaks Creole with her kids, and I guess if none of her neighbors ever talk to her, she doesn't have much chance to practice Spanish.

"Thank you for coming," she says, probably thinking my father has sent me to ask after her oldest son.

I smile like she's right. I wish she were. That would be much better than coming to tell her younger son that I can't teach him bike mechanics anymore. I've tried for two days now to think of another place to continue the lessons, but every one of them is too visible or too far from the clinic.

At some point, I decided *to hell with my parents*, grabbed the green bike and rode it partway down the hill to Nerick's place. But then Dad appeared out of nowhere and said that if I didn't get the bike back to the clinic within three minutes, he wouldn't let me touch the bikes again for the rest of the summer. I haven't ridden either bike since.

"How is Wilkens?" I ask Nerick's mother.

"Better, *gracias*." She kisses me on both cheeks, beckons me into the cookshack and calls to one of her daughters to bring me a chair. "Sorry. I keep stirring or lunch will burn. You stay for lunch? No? Okay. Yes, Wilkens much better. He works again, *gracias a Diós*. Gracias to your father too!"

We stumble through a conversation about the dangers of farmwork and how great it would be to have a medical clinic all year long, not just in the summer when my parents are here. She says that Aracely's abuela is getting old and can't travel to heal people as much as she used to. "And Aracely sells herbs at the market. Doesn't give them. Different from her grandmother. My sons say this is the future. No more old ways."

It's funny to think of Aracely as a trendsetter, someone breaking tradition. "Do you think a person could make a good living from the herbs?" I ask. "Selling them at the market, I mean?"

Nerick's mom laughs. "Who here make good living? Aracely will survive. Like everybody."

But will she be happy? I want to ask. *And are you happy? Do you regret getting married now that your husband's gone and left you?*

"Hola!" When Nerick sticks his head into the cookshack, I'm perched on the little wooden chair his sister brought me, my eyes watering from the woodsmoke of the cookfire—so much for looking stylish—but he doesn't seem to notice my watery eyes or my clothes, for that matter. "Did you come to see about Wilkens? He's back at work, you know."

"Yes, your mother was telling me. That's fantastic!" I smile, but the smoke in my eyes is really getting to me now. I stand up and say I should go.

Nerick's mother kisses me on both cheeks again. "Thank you for coming." Her eyes hold mine, and I resist the urge to squirm. I don't feel like I deserve such a welcome when I should have been a better friend to Nerick all along and when I've only come now to tell him the bike lessons are over.

He walks with me to the road. I only have a few seconds left to do what I came here for in the first place, and I don't know how.

"You haven't been coming to the market on Saturdays," Nerick says before I can get a word out, and I don't know what to say. Two Saturdays have passed since he first asked about the market. I thought he'd let it go and mind his own business, but I guess not. I'm about to make my usual excuse about being busy, but his eyes meet mine with the same unwavering look his mother has. I can't lie to him.

"You don't talk about Aracely either," he says. "Did you fight?"

I chew on my cheek. I know better than to answer his question, even if I can't see anyone else around. The last thing my ruined friendship needs now is a stream of gossip trailing behind it. But this is Nerick, the closest thing I have to a friend right now. I'm sick of talking to myself. I nod, and I expect him to murmur and say it's a shame. I'll shrug, find a way to tell him what my parents have decided about the bikes, then head up the hill for supper.

"Do you want to talk about it?" he asks.

I swallow hard. That is exactly what my grandmother would say. She would motion to the big
armchair in her living room, and I would flop
down into it and tell her all my problems, and
when I was finished, she'd ask a single question
that would get me talking all over again, usually
solving at least some of the problems I'd sat down
with in the first place.

Suddenly I miss Grandma so much that I've got
tears in my eyes. I fake a coughing fit so I'll have
some excuse for them, and I'm sure he sees through
it, but he doesn't say anything, just asks if I have
time to sit by the river for a bit.

I know I shouldn't. Here, girls my age don't go
places with guys, and if anyone sees us, the news will
travel fast enough to put instant messaging to shame.
I'll go from marimacho to slut in record time.

Screw them, I think. Nerick is the only person
in this whole country who cares how I feel about
anything. Why shouldn't I talk to him?

We turn onto the same small dirt path that
Aracely and I went down two weeks ago. I half
expect to find her here, yanking up clumps of berro,
glaring at me with more anger in her eyes than I'd
ever imagined.

At the river's edge, Nerick sits down on a rock and pokes a stick at the mud below. "What happened?"

I tell him my parents offered to bring her to Canada to study and she decided against it. "I don't know why. I think I told her too much about how Canada is different from here, and it scared her." (I don't mention the marriage. Aracely wanted it to be a secret, and no one's going to hear it from my mouth, even if all the village gossips are already speculating.)

He drops his stick down into the mud and wraps his arms around his tucked-up knees. "Aracely doesn't scare so easily, you know. Think of her selling herbs at the market and going against her abuela like that. *I* wouldn't want to go against her abuela."

I laugh. Abuela is a pretty fierce person. She only comes up to my shoulder, but one look from her stops most people in their tracks. Aracely and I have spent a lot of time trying to win her hugs and avoid those freezing looks. I wonder how Aracely is braving those looks now.

"So you don't think Aracely's too scared to come to Canada?" I ask.

"I don't know," Nerick says. "Maybe she's more afraid of what she'd be leaving behind than what she'd be going to. If she went, she'd never get to see her little sisters and brother grow up. She'd miss her cousin's kids. She wouldn't be with her abuela when she passes on. Not everyone wants to miss out on those things." His voice is bitter as he says the last part, and I bet he's thinking of his dad.

He's never talked to me about his father, and if we'd been behind the school, working on the bikes, or even in his front yard, I might have let the comment slide, but down here at the river, it's kind of echoing between us. "I'm sorry about your dad, Nerick."

He shrugs. "That's just the way it is."

I nod and don't know what else to say. Maybe there *is* nothing else to say.

He jumps off the rock and squelches across the mud to a little patch of dry ground. He picks up a few stones and tosses them into the current one at a time. "Decent people don't leave family behind like they're ashamed of where they come from."

As he talks, I realize he'll never forgive anyone who leaves this place. For him, the person who leaves is just as much a traitor as his father is.

"She'll find a way to make it here, Dian, just like I will." He shoots me a grin. "Someday when I'm a rich bike mechanic, I'll buy my family some land and we'll build a big house, and you'll be welcome to visit anytime."

I feel like he's grabbed my insides and twisted them. I look down at my hands. "Nerick, about the bikes—we can't work on them behind the clinic anymore." I tell him what my parents said and how I've been trying to think of another place but can't come up with one.

"I could come at night," he says, "after everyone's gone home."

Why didn't I think of that? Maybe because no one goes anywhere at night. Not usually anyway. Guys might go to the colmado to play dominoes and drink rum, but only if they live close by. No one would consider walking all the way up the hill at night if they lived at the bottom of it. Some people still talk about the *ciguapa*, a woman whose feet point backward and who roams the countryside after dark to lure people stupid enough to be out at night.

If Nerick comes in the evenings, my parents might be in the room while we work on the bikes. I'll feel awkward, maybe even tongue-tied, and they'll hear every word we say.

"What about the ciguapa?" I ask.

He smirks at me in a way that says he doesn't believe in that stuff. "It's a risk I'm willing to take."

Ten

On Sunday mornings, my parents and I tidy the clinic while upbeat, cheery church songs drift over from across the road. Cucubano doesn't have a church or even a priest who comes regularly, but on Sunday mornings people gather in the warehouse across from the clinic, push the piles of coffee sacks off to the side and set up a few wooden benches and student desks brought over from the school. A village elder decides which songs they'll sing, and they sing all morning.

We never go. Everyone's been inviting us for years, especially since the nearest priest is the one who invited us here. My parents have pointed out that we aren't Catholic, though, so everyone assumes we're Evangelical—the only other religion here that most people have heard of—and they leave us alone.

The truth is that my parents don't believe in God, but announcing that here would be like saying they dance with the Devil every night.

I'm not sure what I believe. I hate the idea of a god who lets so many people suffer, but then again, sometimes I think believing in God would be a relief. (I just failed my math test? Oh, it must be the will of God. My bike got stolen? Hmm. I guess God wanted me to have a different one.) I told this to Aracely once, and she laughed and said it doesn't work that way. She said it's more like knowing that your parents love you and trusting them to always make the best decisions for you. I told her she must trust her parents more than I trust mine, and she was horrified until I pretended that I was joking.

She invited me to church in the warehouse the next Sunday, and I went because I was curious and because I loved the happy music. The music was so cheery that I couldn't help tapping my toes. I didn't know the lyrics, but I hummed along and listened. I decided the words made Christianity sound like a sweet deal, and I wondered if my parents would let me keep going to church. But then an old guy got up to talk about the Bible. For what seemed like forever, he rambled on about why women are weaker than men. I stared at him. I stole glances at the other people sitting there to see if they were as horrified as I was, but everyone was smiling and nodding.

By the time he finally sat down, I'd invented a whole story about how this old guy was a bit loopy and no one had the heart to tell him to sit down and be quiet. But later, I asked Aracely about what he'd said, and she got a confused look on her face. "That's what it says in the Bible. We've just got to accept it. It's part of God's way of testing us."

I looked at her with wide eyes and said I didn't think I'd be going back to the coffee warehouse on Sundays. She looked disappointed. "I guess it's very different from your church."

I nodded and prayed to whatever power might exist that she wouldn't ask me about my church, and in the end she didn't. Why ask about something you think is all wrong anyway?

I could never be part of a religion that tells women they're weak. But whenever I hear the happy music, I wonder if I'm missing something about religion. How is it that people here can have so little and sound so joyful? And it's not just on Sundays either. Every day of the week, people here seem more ready to smile or laugh or even dance than most people I know in Canada. I want some of what they have, and I wish my parents could get some too. I think it would do us all good to quit trying to fix the world and actually enjoy it for once.

This morning, on the second-last Sunday of July, I'm slapping my broom against the fence, watching puffs of orange dust float up. Across the road, the warehouse door is open, and for a moment, the air is silent. I picture an old guy talking—a different old guy, because the one I listened to died a few years ago. Then the place bursts into the last song of the morning.

Normally, this is followed by the scraping of desks against concrete as people get up, and lots of talking, but this time the air goes quiet again for a few moments. Then everyone cheers, and suddenly people are pouring out of the warehouse with big grins on their faces.

Aracely emerges in the middle of the crowd, people kissing her cheeks and hugging her close.

"Please come to our house to celebrate!" her father shouts above the noise. He turns and waves me toward him. "You're all welcome."

By this time, my parents have come out of the clinic and are standing next to me. "What's all that about?"

A group of kids skips past. "*Se caaaaaaaasa* Araceeeeely! Araceeeeely's getting maaaaaaaarried!"

Aracely must have heard from Vin that he's found a job at the mine. The engagement is now official. I feel like someone's just taken a year off my life. Or maybe about thirty years off Aracely's.

"You coming?" shouts Orlando, the owner of the colmado.

I think I'm going to throw up, but before I can turn and run, my mother's arm is around my shoulders, holding me tight. "We'll change our clothes and be right there!" she shouts and herds me into the school.

Dad follows, and when he closes the door behind us, I stare at them. "You don't seriously expect—"

"Yes." Mom's rummaging in her suitcase. "We're going to the party, and so are you."

Dad shrugs and looks sorry. Like he totally understands what I'm going through but can't possibly do anything about it. I'm about to tell them what they can do with their party when Mom turns on me. "We didn't come here to offend people, Dian, and you know that's exactly what'll happen if we don't go. I'm not going to go alone and answer everyone's questions about why Aracely's best friend decided not to come to the engagement party." She tosses me a purple skirt and white blouse I've never seen before but that are reasonably presentable. I consider laying the clothes on the bed and sitting down and refusing to budge, like Gandhi at a demonstration, but my father clears his throat.

"What your mother is trying to say," he says, a change of pants in one hand and a shirt in the other, "is that you need to choose your method of protest. Sometimes a boycott is the best approach. Other times, you need to show solidarity, convince people from the inside. This, I think, is one of those times."

His voice is soft, and when I raise my eyes to meet his, the helpless-parent look isn't there. He looks like he really means what he just said.

I glare at him but pick up the skirt and blouse and put them on.

❧

Merengue music is blaring from Orlando's battery-powered ghetto blaster, and people are spilling out onto the road when we arrive. We greet people as if we haven't seen each other in weeks, and everyone pushes us toward the bride-to-be and her family to congratulate them.

Aracely is standing by the door of the house. Her hair is pulled back, and she's smiling a close-lipped smile, eyes averted, as the Eye raves on about something. Aracely's eyes flicker up; she sees me staring at her, and she looks away again, like I'm invisible.

So much for convincing from the inside. The only thing I've achieved by coming here is feeling like a worthless friend.

Aracely's younger sister offers me a glass of pop, which I take even though I hate the stuff. The bubbles make my nose itch, but I'm grateful for the glass right now. It gives me somewhere to look and something to do with my hands. "Gracias," I say, and Cecilia smiles and hurries away.

I look around for my parents or a group of kids that I could pretend to be looking after—at least I'd feel useful and occupied—but the kids are running around, dodging between people's legs, and even I know I'm too old for that.

"Thank you for coming," Aracely says, and I jump. She laughs—laughs the way she used to before Vin proposed, and for a moment I think she's forgiven me, but of course it has nothing to do with me and everything to do with the entire village crowded around us within earshot of our conversation.

I wish I'd thought about what to say when I saw her. I'm a terrible actor, and if I say any of the usual things—*congratulations, I'm so happy for you*—everyone will know I don't mean it and the gossips will be on high alert. If Cucubano had a newspaper, the headline would read *Bride's Best Friend Disdains Marriage Plans*, and it would ruin any chances I have left of swaying Aracely.

"So he got a job at the mine then?" I force a smile.

"He sent a letter all about it. Come with me. I'll show it to you."

A few feet behind her, the Eye glances up from her conversation and looks at me. I beam at Aracely as if we've never exchanged an angry word in our lives, and I link my arm with hers. I don't believe for a minute that she'll show me Vin's letter. I bet she wants to get away from this crowd, and if she wants to use me as an excuse, I'm fine with that. It's not like I wanted to be here in the first place.

She leads me into the house, where kids are playing hide-and-seek. She lifts the edge of a mattress in the corner and shoos some of the kids away.

"Oooh. Aracely needs privacy to read her *love* letter," her brother teases.

"Go on, Miguel," Aracely says. "Take the kids outside. I want to talk to Dian."

Miguel shepherds the kids out. Aracely opens the envelope and we sit on the bed together. She makes no move to pull out the letter though. "The Eye was warning me about you back there."

"What?" I have no idea what she's talking about.

"She says Nerick's been visiting you at night."

The light is dim and I can't read her face, but she sounds hurt. Why would she be hurt though? It's not like she's going out of her way to be my friend these days, so what right does she have to be jealous of my friendship with Nerick?

She can't possibly be thinking it's any *more* than friendship because she knows I share a bedroom with my parents, and they're home when he comes over. And I'm sure she's not going weird because of the Haitian thing, either, because she's always treated him well. *If I've learned one thing from having a big scar across my face, it's that you can't judge a person by how he looks*, she says. So what on earth is her problem?

I try hard not to sound annoyed as I explain to her about the bike-repair lessons. "My parents are there the whole time. They open the door to him, and they don't ever leave while he's there. I bet the Eye knows all that too." I imagine her peering out from behind the shutters of her house. It's the only house in the whole of Cucubano that has windows—no glass, which is too expensive, but openings and shutters. Dad says it must get awfully cold in there because the shutters allow too much heat to escape, but I'm sure she doesn't care as long as she can still watch from inside every move others make.

But, of course, she can't see *everything* from in there. She can't see how Nerick's too busy memorizing every detail of the bicycle to even have time for talking. She can't see how my parents look up from their medical journals every now and then to watch us. They offer us snacks or tea partway through the evening, but Nerick always refuses, not wanting to waste a single minute of bicycle time. He's polite enough to chat at the beginning and end of his stay, telling us about his family and the odd jobs he's managed to find, but that's as deep and personal as it gets. I'm totally fine with that. I think it's hilarious, though, that the Eye has invented a big Romeo and Juliet love story when nothing could be further from the truth. "So he comes over in the evenings," I say. "How can she possibly think that's enough to convince people that we're—"

"She saw you going down to the river with him, Dian."

I wince. So much for anyone in Cucubano ever having any respect for me again. Like I said, girls never spend time alone with guys before getting married. Dates are chaperoned. Girls are supposed to arrive at their weddings without ever having been kissed. Aracely was appalled when I told her what North American teenagers get up to. And now everyone for miles around will be talking about what a slut I am. Somehow that bugs me even more than the whole marimacho thing. At least it's *true* that I like to climb trees and swim in the river. I'm the very furthest thing from a slut.

"She told me to stay away from you." Aracely whispers and holds both of my hands, like friends here often do. "I mean, she's told me that before too, but that was because she was afraid I'd turn into a marimacho. Now she says being seen with you could ruin my reputation."

I gape at her. The world's turned inside out, and nothing makes sense anymore. How can everyone be happy to marry off a fifteen-year-old and at the same time hate me for talking to Nerick?

Aracely squeezes my hands. "I don't believe any of it, but I thought you should know what people are saying."

I want to tell her I don't care, that I won't be around long enough for it to matter to me, but we'd both know I was lying. I can fly all the way to Canada and beyond, and I'll still take these stories with me. I'll think about them and wonder if I should have been more careful, should have thought more about where I was and who I was with and how my actions might affect Aracely, before I went down to the river with Nerick. I went because I needed someone to talk to, but I should have cared more about the consequences.

"So will you have to avoid me now?" I try to make my voice sound casual, joking. It's kind of an ironic question since we were barely on speaking terms until a few minutes ago.

Aracely opens her mouth just as someone cranks up Orlando's ghetto blaster. The song is one of Aracely's favorites. For a moment, she looks at me, considering. Then she links her arm with mine. "Let's go, Dian. Let's dance."

Arm in arm, we step out into the sunshine. I raise my head to match the proud, unabashed tilt of hers.

Eleven

"Dian, we'd like to talk to you."

Mom and Dad are sitting on the edge of the bottom bunk. It's the end of July, about a week after Aracely's engagement party, and I'm sweeping the floor where Nerick and I dismantled a bike wheel an hour ago. Usually, by this time, my parents are making a few final notes in their medical journals and getting ready to turn out the light. Tonight, though, they sit staring at me, wide awake.

I lean the broom against the wall and dust off my hands. "What is it?"

My parents glance at each other. Dad nudges Mom's foot with his. Mom takes a deep breath. "We'd like to ask you about Nerick."

I feel a tingle of dread but tell myself not to worry. Even if the Eye has said something to them, they know me well enough to understand that he and I are just friends. Maybe they want to hear his plans for the future, to see if there's any way they can help him like they were going to help Aracely.

Mom leans her elbows on her knees and smiles the way I imagine she smiles at her patients— a confident, trustworthy smile. "We want to hear how things are going."

I shrug. "You heard what he was saying about Wilkens maybe leaving for the city. Nerick'll have to work twice as hard until his brother gets a city job. So they could use some help, if that's what you're getting at."

"Mm." Dad nods. Mom sits waiting, like she expects me to say more.

"He misses his father a lot," I offer. "He doesn't talk about it much, but I think he's still pretty angry at him for leaving, and I bet he's afraid his brother will do the same thing now—take off and never come back."

More nods. More awkward silence.

"Dian," Dad says, "you know you can come to us about anything, right? Anytime you need help or support."

"You're growing up now," Mom adds. "You're reaching an age of experimentation, and it's perfectly natural to—"

Oh god. "You've been talking to the—to Miralis Vargas, haven't you?" My voice is angry, what I'm sure my mother would call *argumentative*, but what do they expect? Are they honestly worried about the rumors the Eye is spreading?

"No, no," Dad says too quickly. "I mean, we haven't been talking to her any more than usual. But we've been hearing some things in general that we weren't aware of. About you and Nerick."

I close my eyes. This whole conversation is making me very tired—tired of being in a place I never wanted to come to, tired of people spreading lies about me and, most of all, tired of my parents not having a clue about who I really am and what I want.

"…come to us about anything," Mom is saying. "*Anything* you need."

The way she says *anything* makes it clear she's not talking about only spiritual guidance. They keep a big box of contraceptives in a corner of the clinic. They bring it every year, just in case someone shows an interest. And now the town gossip's convinced them that their thirteen-year-old daughter should be their next candidate for birth control.

"You think I'm having sex with Nerick."

My mother's cheeks turn first-aid-kit red, Dad passes a hand over his eyes and won't look at me, and some part of me is marveling that I managed to say the words *sex* and *Nerick* in the same sentence without choking in embarrassment. The tired numbness I felt a few seconds ago is totally gone. "You're worried Miralis Vargas knows more about your daughter than you do."

Dad's head snaps up. Mom places a hand on his knee. "I don't want to talk about Miralis right now," she tells him. "I want to talk about Dian."

Dad looks down again, fuming at the floor. Then he takes a deep breath and stretches his legs, and I can almost hear the clunk of his thoughts shifting gears. "It's not like we believed the gossip hook, line and sinker, you know." He gives me a half smile, as if this is all quite funny, and I see where he's going with this. Chapter two of *Raising a Confident Teenager* recommends injecting humor whenever possible. Catching more flies with honey than with vinegar or something. Someone should tell Dad that humor doesn't work if he's clearly terrified that the joke might be the truth.

But Dad hasn't clued into that detail, and he keeps talking. "One of our patients warned us about your relationship with Nerick. The way this person told it, you'd be pregnant by the end of the summer, and we'd be bringing Nerick home with us as the father of our grandchild!" Dad forces out a laugh, and his eyes are begging me to laugh too. Beside him, Mom doesn't crack a smile. She's staring at me as if her eyes could bore into me and let the bad spirits out, like doctors in the Middle Ages did with crazy people.

The whole situation is so ridiculous that part of me would like to laugh with my father. We'd be laughing for different reasons, but I'm not sure he'd notice.

I stay silent. None of this feels like it has anything to do with me. It's all about my parents—who don't know me at all—and the Eye, who has too much time on her hands and hates either me or Nerick or both of us.

"Dian?"

They're both looking at me. "Aren't you going to say anything?" Dad asks.

"What do you want me to say?"

Mom frowns. "We're here to listen, Dian."

"Really?" I stalk across the room and snatch a water bottle, toothpaste and toothbrush from the teacher's desk. "If you're here to listen, then how could you possibly think I'm having sex when I've spent the whole summer talking about Aracely having to grow up too soon?"

They at least have the decency to look embarrassed. Neither of them looks at me as I head for the door. I pull it open, step into the darkness and wave across the road at the Eye in case she's peeping through the slats of her shutters in my direction. Behind me, my parents say something, but I'm not sure what, because I spend almost an hour outside looking at the stars. I don't go back inside until the light's off and I can hear them snoring.

❧

I wake that night to the sound of sniffling. I can't recognize whose it is because neither of my parents ever cries. I hear the squeak of the bunk beds as someone gets up and then my dad's voice.

"…be okay…be okay." I don't know if he's saying he'll be okay, or if he's telling Mom she will be.

When I was little, I had nightmares. My parents would take turns sleeping beside me to scare the monsters away. Mom gave me a superhero anti-monster ring. Dad gave me a book about a brave princess who outsmarted a dragon to save her best friend. They both sang me lullabies.

Here, in the darkness, I want them to sing me lullabies again, to say that everything will be all right, that nothing will ever scare us again.

Instead, I've become *their* monster. And I've got a whole slew of my own.

Twelve

It's dawn, and my parents are still snoring when I get up. I push away the mosquito netting, reach out with one arm to grab my slippers, flip them upside down and shake them. When no flash-drive-size cockroaches come ka-thunking out, I swing out of bed, shake my clothes and get dressed.

I feel like I haven't slept at all. My brain feels foggy, and I'm convinced I'm a terrible person. I'm angry at my parents and angry at myself for being angry. Everyone loves them. This village depends on them. The future of the world depends on people like them. And sometimes I hate them for all that. I wish they'd just ignore

the world, make a cup of hot (fair-trade) choco-
late with me, and sit and talk, like Grandma does.

I wish I were the kind of person who brought
that out in them. Instead, I make them suspicious.
I scare them. I make them cry.

If we go through breakfast pretending nothing
happened last night, though, I'm going to scream.

I grab a cloth bag, drop in a water bottle and some
of the fruit we keep in a big plastic box, and tiptoe
over to the teacher's desk to find a pen and paper.
*Good morning. I woke up early and wanted to go for
a walk. I'll be back in time to make lunch. And don't
worry. I'm not visiting Nerick. D.*

I know they wouldn't want me to go, that they'll
spend the whole morning freaking out about where I
might be and what kind of trouble I might be getting
into. But I'm hoping that by lunchtime, I'll either
know what to say to them or, more likely, they'll be
so full of stories of what *could* have happened to me
that they won't be waiting for me to say anything.

∼

It's not our place anymore, not one we share.
I came here because I knew it would be too early

for Aracely. Right now, she's probably at home, cleaning up after breakfast and starting preparations for lunch. But even without her here, this is her place. Her herbs—even more of them now—are hanging from the ceiling. Her altar is still in one corner, her drawing book on the table in the other. The floor is swept clean. I thought I'd find solitude, but now I feel like I'm torturing myself with one more place I don't belong.

I'm sitting in the middle of the floor, arms wrapped tight around my knees, when she comes in. The light behind her marks the curves of her body, and if I didn't know, I'd think she was a grown woman. This will be her house one day, and she will come through this very door, in just the same way, to be with her husband, her children and maybe, someday, her grandchildren. This is where she most wants to be in the world. Her forever place. I don't know what it feels like to have a place like that.

"Dian?" She smiles like she's not at all surprised to see me.

"Sorry. I wasn't going to touch anything. I just wanted—"

"It's okay." She sits down beside me. "What's up?"

I hesitate. Can I really complain about anything in my privileged life when she might be married and pregnant at this time next year? And how can I go on about my own stuff when my reputation is causing *her* problems?

I think about getting up, apologizing again and leaving, but when I look at her face, it's the same Aracely who sat here with me last summer, the same one who listened to me, and laughed with me, and shared all her own secrets. She's the same person who was going to come to Canada and be my best friend forever, even if all that's changed now.

I tell her about my parents. She listens, winces in all the right places, and when I'm finished, she says, "I can't believe it. Don't they know you at all?"

I shrug. "They think they do. They ask what I think about stuff all the time, but every time my opinion is different from theirs, they assume I don't know what I'm talking about. And they never ask how I *feel*. What I feel doesn't matter at all. It's what the rest of the world is going through that's really important."

She looks at me without saying anything for a second. Then she says, "I'm sorry, Dian. I wish none of this had happened."

"Me too." I wish Aracely was still coming to Canada. I wish the Eye would get a life and stop inventing stories about everyone else's. I wish my parents still listened to me like they did when I was five, instead of going through the motions.

"And you know you can come here whenever you want, right?" She waves a hand at the herbs and at the walls around us. "It's good to have friends here. It keeps the house happy."

I laugh. "I'm not sure how happy the house is to have me here, all angry and frustrated."

"It's all part of life," she says, and for some reason I remember the drawing she did of herself and Vin in front of this house. All part of life. Her life. The life that she's chosen. The image of that life isn't so shocking to me anymore. It feels kind of inevitable. I hope she can be happy.

And as I look at her smiling back at me, I want to believe that there's no reason why she *wouldn't* be happy. She is the same strong, passionate, adventurous Aracely I've always known.

She gets up and goes over to a bundle of herbs hanging in the far corner. "I came to get some ruda for my cousin. She's run out."

I get up too and dust myself off. "I'm glad you came," I say. I want to tell her I've missed her, but I can't bring myself to say it. I don't want her to whip around and remind me that I'm the one who started fighting with her. She told me her plans, and I got mad.

Every time my opinion is different from theirs, they assume I don't know what I'm talking about.

I was describing my parents, but I might as well have been describing how I'd treated Aracely when I found out about Vin.

"I'm sorry, Aracely. About everything I said, and making you mad, and hurting your feelings."

She scans my face, and this time I guess she can see that I mean it. "I'm glad I came too," she says.

I walk with her as far as her cousin's. She asks me if I'm free on Saturday to help her bring herbs to market.

I smile, and she laughs. "And guess what? If you promise to behave yourself, and if you stop taking off down to the river with boys, I might be willing to learn a few words of English. I'll butcher the language so badly that you'll ask me to stop anyway."

I grin, and I'm still smiling as I cross the beet field and step between the coffee trees of the cafetál. I don't know how Aracely and I can be so different and so close at the same time.

It's wonderful, though, that it *is* possible.

❧

"You should be ashamed of yourself."

If I were standing, Miralis Vargas would only come up to my nose, but right now the Eye is towering over me, Aracely and Nerick. We're arranging bundles of herbs on a mat on the ground at the Saturday market, and she's blocking out the sun, hands on hips, scowling at me.

"I thought you'd be more careful, now that everyone's talking. And you, Aracely, I thought you had better sense than to keep their company."

Aracely is on her feet before I can make sense of what's happening. She steps over the mat like she's ready to pounce, but when she opens her mouth, her voice is sweet, almost childlike. "Yes, it's strange how people are talking, don't you think? The person who started the stories clearly knows nothing about Dian or Nerick, or about their friendship. That person invented all sorts of details. Who would be so mean, do you think?"

Nerick's behind Aracely now, arms crossed, and I stand too, readying myself for whatever might happen next.

The Eye's face turns a funny shade of red, and she balls her hands into fists, but she can't accuse Aracely of disrespect without admitting to having started the rumors.

"I've always hated rumors," says Nerick. "When my father left, someone told all sorts of stories about where he had gone and why. Not a single one of them was ever true."

"How do you know that?" the Eye snaps.

"I asked around," Nerick says. "Every time I heard something, I got all excited that this time it might be the truth. It never mattered to me how terrible the story was. I thought that if it had even a speck of truth, it could help me get my dad back. That's all I cared about. And with every new story, I got my hopes up, but every time, I found out that the rumor couldn't be true for one reason or another. It's a terrible thing to spread lies and make a bad situation even worse."

I imagine Nerick at twelve, ripped apart by his father leaving and ripped apart again every time a new story flew around.

"Well," the Eye says, "people will talk. It's the human condition, I guess. The less you give people to talk about, the less gossip you'll have to worry about."

"Not necessarily," I say. "Some people have such wild imaginations that they'll invent things where nothing exists at all."

This time, the Eye glares at me openly, so I glare right back. Let her talk. I'll be gone soon enough anyway. That's what I figure.

Thirteen

I'm not coming back next summer. Not a chance. Not when Aracely's married and maybe pregnant. Not when Nerick already knows everything I can teach him about bicycles and won't come by anymore. (Even if he wanted to, I doubt he'd visit, knowing how much fuss it causes.) Surely my parents will understand how torturous it would be for me to come back next summer.

It's the second week of August, and next week we'll start packing for the trip home. I'll mention something to my parents about saying my final goodbyes, making it very clear that I mean *final*. I'll present it like a done deal: I'm not coming back next summer, and it isn't up for discussion at any family meeting.

In seventeen days, I'll be riding my bike again. Or visiting Emily. Or stirring compost with my grandmother. I won't be sweeping orange dust off the concrete floor of the bedroom I share with my parents.

"Can I come in?"

Aracely's leaning against the door frame, her head tilted toward it, smiling. But her voice is tight, and her eyebrows are pulled together as if she might cry.

I wave her in and close the door behind her. "What's up?"

Her smile disintegrates, and she perches on the edge of my bed. "Vin's grandmother came by this morning." She falters, and tears stream down her face.

I picture Vin lying in hospital, his eyes burned out by toxic mining chemicals. Or his skin disfigured, or a limb gone, or...or...

Aracely waves away the panic that must be showing in my face. "Don't worry. He's fine."

I reconfigure Vin into the happy guy in the drawings. "Oh. What happened then?"

Aracely stares at the floor, hands clasped in her lap. "His grandmother doesn't want me spending time with you and Nerick anymore."

"What!" I exclaim. "You're not married yet! She can't tell you how to spend your time." I want to ask what on earth Aracely's thinking, marrying into such a nosy and controlling family, but that's a whole different discussion—one way too similar to the argument we've been having all summer long, and I don't want to go there now.

"Too many people are talking, Dian." The tears have stopped now, and she's looking at me as if she's asking for something. "Vin's grandmother says people might turn against me too, and that would reflect badly on our marriage. She wants—"

"What? For you to give up the right to choose your own friends? To ditch me and Nerick because an old gossip who lives across the road from us has nothing better to do than make up stories?" I'm standing in front of her, fists clenched. "What does she want, Aracely?"

I try to calm down, without much success. After weeks of trying to figure out how to stop the marriage, *now* I find out that I only had to go down to the river to talk to Nerick and all bets would be off? How ridiculous is that?

"I don't want to stop talking to you, Dian," Aracely says. "You're my friend. But you'll leave at the end of the summer, and I imagine you won't be coming back. Not for a long time anyway."

Her eyes meet mine, and ice water trickles down my back. She knows. I never said a word about not coming back, but she knows.

You could still come to Canada and leave the gossips behind, I think, but the words sound hollow. No matter how much she hates certain things about where she lives, we both know she'd be miserable in Canada. I get that now.

"We have to do something," I say.

She looks up at me with suspicion on her face, but I'm not hiding anything this time. "I'll talk to Vin's grandmother," I say. "No, better yet, my *parents* will talk to her. People still respect them, right? They're the doctors that the priest sent. That's good, isn't it? Even if they're the parents of that terrible girl who talked to Nerick by the river?"

❧

"It's not our place to meddle in people's personal lives," Mom says that evening when I ask her and Dad to visit Vin's grandmother.

It's bedtime. Nerick's come and gone. And even though we're not leaving for another two weeks, my bags are all packed. I needed time to think, and organizing stuff always makes me feel better. I've even taken a stab at organizing my parents' things.

My parents must have noticed all this premature packing, but they haven't said anything. Mom's sitting at the teacher's desk, her finger marking a line in a medical journal that she is reading. My dad's lying in bed making notes in his day planner. I can't believe he uses a day planner in a place like Cucubano. I think this is part of my family's problem. At least he has the decency to put down his pen and look at me.

"Our job here is to offer help where people want it," he says, "and if they don't ask for help, we keep our noses out of it. There's a very fine line between support and telling people how to live."

"And you jump over that line all the time." I'm lying in bed, arms crossed, staring at the bunk above me. "You were happy to bring Aracely to Canada with us when you thought it would make you look selfless, but now you can't be bothered to stand up for her in Cucubano. How does that make any sense?"

"Look," Mom says, finally taking her finger out of that damn journal, closing its pages and putting it to one side. "We're not refusing to stand up for her. I just think we can tackle this problem in other ways."

"How?"

My parents glance at each other. Mom nods, and Dad speaks. "If you stop spending so much time with Nerick, this whole thing might blow over on its own. You'll be old news. People will move on to something else."

I turn and stare at him. "You want me to get rid of a friend just so you don't have to stand up for Aracely? You're going to let the old bat across the road *win*?"

Mom shouts my name so loud that even a deaf bat could hear. So much for all my efforts to keep my own voice calm and even.

I grit my teeth. I'm not going to storm out like I usually do. I'm staying. Like my parents do when they're at the Legislature, protesting about the tar sands, or clearcutting, or foreign mining operations, or any of the other bazillion things they're unhappy about. I'll stay here all night if I have to, and I'll tell them I won't go back to Canada until they do what I've asked. That'll throw them for a loop, especially since I've got my bags already packed, two weeks early.

But they need to know I'm serious about this. They need to listen to me, and maybe the only way I can make that happen is to use the same tactics they use against a government they don't agree with.

Protest respectfully and demand respect. How many times have they drilled that into me?

"Don't shout at me, Mom." I sit up in bed and raise my eyebrows at her. "Please."

She narrows her eyes but says nothing, just crosses her arms and looks away. Dad takes the cue. "I'm trying to understand your position," he says. "You do realize that if we talk to Vin's grandmother, we'd actually be *removing* any obstacles to the marriage, right?" He looks at me like I haven't thought this out.

Do not blow up, I tell myself. *Keep calm.* "I'm not totally into underage marriage now, if that's what you're thinking. I'm talking about a person—Aracely—not a protest issue. No matter what I think of her marriage, I'm not just going to sit around while people hurt my friend with a bunch of lies. You might, but I'm not."

"Don't make us out to be the bad guys." Mom's arms are still crossed, and she's still scowling, but she's not shouting anymore. "We're not the ones spreading stories, and we've told you how you can get the stories to stop."

For such brainy and passionate people, they sure abandon their mottos fast when it's convenient. "What happened to *Do what you know is right* and *If you just stand by and watch, you're part of the problem*?"

Mom lets out an exasperated sigh, but Dad is looking thoughtful. I'm halfway there.

"I'm going to bed," Mom says and goes outside to brush her teeth. Dad follows her. I get up to grab a flashlight and sit back down on my bed.

"Good night," my parents say when they come back.

"I don't think we've finished this discussion," I answer.

"Oh, I think we have," Mom says. "We're the parents here. We set the boundaries." She flicks off the light.

She's quoting from *Raising a Confident Teenager*, which she only does when she knows she's on shaky ground. I flick on my flashlight and shine it on their beds.

"Turn that off, Dian. It's time to sleep."

"No," I say. "I'm not sleeping and neither are you until we finish talking about this."

"*Turn off that flashlight.*" That's Mom's furious voice.

I train the beam on her.

Mom flings back the covers. "Give that to me."

I bolt out of bed and start running. I know exactly where the bags are, and I have the flashlight, so I know I won't trip. I shine the light on Mom's face. She looks confused and a little alarmed. *Raising a Confident Teenager* doesn't mention midnight flashlight-tag games at all.

Dad laughs. I shine the flashlight on him. He looks into the darkness in Mom's direction. "I'll race you for her," he tells her, and all of a sudden, we're all dashing around in the semidarkness, falling over suitcases, Mom swearing, and me and Dad laughing. Finally, she makes it to the wall switch and turns on the overhead light.

She's trying to look serious but doing a very bad job of it, standing there in bare feet, yoga pants and a T-shirt that says *I love my chihuahua*. (My mother hates dogs, especially small yappy ones. At least my parents walk their talk when it comes to wearing donation clothes.)

"You ready to talk?" I ask.

"If it means we can eventually sleep after a long day, yes," Mom says.

"I have a feeling," says Dad, "that the lights won't all go out again until we agree to what you've said, Dian. Am I right?"

I nod, not smiling anymore.

"You're a tough negotiator," he says, but he looks more admiring than angry.

"Years of training," I tell him. "I learned from the best."

Fourteen

The Eye rushes past, ignoring us. Technically, Aracely, Nerick and I should be offended, scandalized, outraged, but I can't stop grinning.

"I wish she'd done this sooner," Aracely whispers in my ear.

"Who knew she could keep her mouth shut for this long?" Nerick mutters, and we laugh.

It's the second-last Saturday before I go back to Canada, and we're each carrying stuff home from the market. My friends have groceries. I have paper, pencils, an eraser and envelopes that I'll leave in Aracely's house with some money for postage. I'll hide them, so she doesn't find them until after we leave Cucubano. (She'd object to the money for postage, but I know she doesn't have money to spare.) I've already explained how to call me collect from the public phone in the next village over, if ever they need to. I doubt they'll call, but I feel better knowing it's possible.

"What on earth did your parents tell her?" Nerick asks me when the Eye is far ahead of us. A warm breeze ruffles the tall grasses on either side of the pavement, and we walk on the gravelly edge of the road, ready to jump aside if a truck comes roaring past.

I shrug. "My parents talked to Vin's grandmother. Then they all went to talk to the Eye. Apparently, she got hopping mad but didn't deny anything. Dad tells the story like a huge triumph. Mom's worried the Eye will turn everyone against us now."

Nerick shakes his head. "Everyone knows what Señora Vargas is like, and no one would let her push away the only two doctors who ever come here. You've been sent by the priest, after all. Señora will be offended for a while, and then everyone will forget this ever happened."

"You'll be old news, Dian," Aracely agrees.

"Thank goodness for that."

Thank goodness, and thank my parents. They did even more than I asked them to. Now there's just one more thing I want them to do before we go.

❧

Their favorite quote is from Gandhi: *First they ignore you, then they laugh at you, then they fight you, then you win.*

I'm at the second-last stage right now. I sit cross-legged on my bed, as calm as I can be, while my mother fights.

"It's against everything we believe in, Dian!" She pulls up a chair and sits down. "Why do you think we forbade *you* to ride the bikes all summer? We don't believe in one person pedaling around, flaunting something no one else owns."

"But it won't *belong* to Nerick," I say. "He'll use it for deliveries, which means he'll get his work done faster, but mostly he'll use it to teach bike mechanics to anyone who wants to learn."

Mom sighs. We've been over this several times now—my plans, how I'm sure they'll work, and how she disagrees. (I think I've almost convinced Dad though. Right now, he's sitting at the teacher's desk with a pad of paper, thinking about how to pull this off.) "Look," Mom says, "I know you'll do everything in your power to collect bikes and raise money to send them here. I know people have done this kind of thing before, but it could take years. And meanwhile, Nerick will be pedaling around, the only person in the village with a bicycle, and we'll look like we've favored him above anyone else in Cucubano."

"But we aren't just giving him a bike," I say. "He's *earned* it. No one else wanted to learn to fix bicycles, even after Señora Vargas made sure everyone knew I was giving lessons."

Mom blinks at me, and her exasperation melts into a condescending tenderness. "Oh, Dian. You don't really think Nerick only came to learn about bicycles, do you?"

I feel my cheeks blazing hot, and I can't look at her. Of course by now I've figured out that he likes me. As much as I like him. But what's the use of thinking about that when we live an entire continent apart, and a whole village flies into panic if we even talk to each other?

My mother's gazing at me like I still believe in Santa Claus. I hate how she assumes she knows far more than I ever will, and how it never occurs to her that I might know something she doesn't. I'd love to tell her about the cycle-tourism guy just to wipe that condescending look off her face, but if Nerick wants to keep it quiet, so will I.

"The point, Mom, is that anyone could have asked to learn. They didn't. Nerick did. End of story." I cross my arms and try to snatch back the meditative calm I had a few minutes ago. "It sounds like you're worried about what people will think if you give Nerick a chance."

"No," she says, "this is *not* about Nerick being Haitian, if that's what you're thinking. This is about beliefs and what we stand for. This has nothing to do with Nerick specifically."

"And that's why it's so unfair!" I say. "He worked hard this summer. He actually cares about the bicycles, so why not give him one so he can teach everyone when the other bikes get here?"

Mom passes a hand over her face, like she's trying to reason with a toddler. Dad looks at me, concerned. Everything is riding on this one moment. If I don't say something brilliant right now, both bikes will be tossed into the back of a pickup truck and carted off to the city next Wednesday. Nerick will forget most of what he's learned by the time the cycle-tourism guy comes back. *If* he comes back. This bike, and the other bikes we'll send later on, could change my friend's future—and the futures of plenty of people in the village—forever. Nerick, the most knowledgeable bike mechanic in a village full of bicycles, could earn enough to keep food on his family's table no matter what color his skin is, and no one would depend on the whims of a random rich, foreign cyclist.

"One of the best ways you can help Nerick," Mom says, "is to help him stay off of Miralis Vargas's radar. Giving him the only bicycle in the village would be like painting a target on his back, as far as rumors are concerned."

She's right, of course. And I hate that. Why should someone as awful as the Eye have so much power?

"What if we get her involved?" Dad asks. "Miralis Vargas, I mean."

Mom and I both look at him like he's insane. I picture the Eye flying down the road on a bicycle, shouting her rumors at top volume, like the town crier. She'd crash for sure.

"She can be the spokesperson, if you'll pardon the pun." Dad beams at us and pauses in case we laugh, but when neither of us does, he carries on. "Every campaign needs a voice, right? She's perfect for it."

"Except that she might spread a story that's completely different from what we tell her," Mom says.

Dad's smile droops.

"What if we give her a job or something?" I ask. "What if she's the official list-keeper of who will get bicycles? She'd love that—people coming to her place to have their names written down on a list. I bet she'd stick to the story really well if she were one of the main characters."

Dad smiles again. Mom hesitates, and I'm afraid she's going to come up with another reason why this will never work, but after a few seconds she nods. Dad passes her pen and paper, and we begin to plan.

"Pedal! Go, go, go!" I push the green bike forward. Nerick grips the handlebars like he can squeeze them into obedience, and he wobbles ahead on the pitted pavement.

I speed-walk behind him and pretend not to see his sisters and mom peeping around the edge of the cookshack. He's so focused on the road that the mountains could sink into the earth and he wouldn't flinch. His knees rise and fall slowly—too slowly—and the bike topples sideways.

He lands on the ground with a thud, and I pull the heavy bike off him. "You okay?"

He dusts himself off. "I liked it better when I was the one teaching you. Are you sure you don't need work on your tree-climbing skills?"

I laugh. "Too bad you couldn't make deliveries from the treetops. You'd be the richest guy in the valley."

He makes a crack about needing to build a slingshot to hurl his deliveries to his clients, climbs onto the bicycle again, pushes off, rides a few meters, falls and does it all over again. Many times. Each time, he stays on the bike a bit longer, but eventually he asks me to ride instead, so he can watch.

I climb on and fly off down the bumpy road, a beacon of yellow tie-dye and red plaid. His sisters and mom come out of hiding and clap. At the bend in the road, I turn and race back, feeling the strength in my pumping legs for the first time in months.

Tomorrow I will stack the plaids, tie-dyes and tacky T-shirts on the teacher's desk, and we'll leave it all behind. In a few days, in the city, I'll pull on a pair of slim-fitting brown shorts and a purple tank top, and I'll tie back my hair at the base of my neck. I will look the way I'd wanted Nerick to see me.

And that will be nothing compared to this: me blasting along the pavement, giving the pedals everything I've got, with Nerick beaming at me and his whole family cheering, not just for this moment but for everything that we can make happen together. This is a memory we'll all carry with us.

This is what I'll take home with me.

Fifteen

The brown paper is worn, the corners are scrunched, and the stamps look faded, exhausted from the two-month journey to get here.

Aracely posted her letter the fifteenth of October. It's December now.

Dear Dian,

Thank you for the paper, envelopes and the money for postage. This is the first letter that I've written to another country, and I've been trying since the day you left to think up stories interesting enough to send. In the end, though, I'll just write what's in my heart. I know you'll be happy to hear from me, no matter what I say.

Things here are the same as always, with a few changes. Lety had another baby. Señor Morales passed away. Guin Sanchez took off for the city, and his wife is relieved, I think.

The market is getting busier for me, as more people are hearing about the herbs. Abuela still hates the idea of me selling them, but life is easier with money, and her complaints are mostly just for show now, I think.

Nerick still helps me bring the herbs to the market, which is kind because he's very busy now, pedaling up the mountain with deliveries, flying down again and teaching people everything he knows about bikes, including how to ride. He's like a different person. He looks people in the eye now, like he never did before.

He picks up the herbs from our house on the bicycle and drops them off at the market for me. We don't talk much, but when we do, he talks about you more than anything. I tease him about it, and he says it's because he spends so much time with the bicycle that he can't help thinking of you. I'm sure that's not the whole story, and since I saw how you two laugh together, I'm sure you share his feelings.

I'm going to finish my letter now because I don't want it to cost too much to send. I hope you had a good trip home. Please say hola to your parents and to Emily

for me, even though I don't know her. You've talked
about her so much that I feel like I do. I miss you.

Saludos,
Aracely

I read the letter a second time, studying the
spots where she scrubbed out her words and
wrote them again. Nowhere does she mention the
Eye, but if Nerick's doing well, I assume the Eye is
keeping quiet.

Aracely hasn't mentioned Vin either. I guess
that means that the marriage is still on, but she
doesn't have any more news about him than when
I left in August.

Brave, I think, as I flop onto our worn couch.
I can't imagine marrying someone I hadn't heard
from for a year. Then again, I can't imagine most of
Aracely's life, even though I've been there with her
every summer for almost as long as I can remember.

I set the letter to one side, kick my feet up and
stretch back. My parents are still at work. I've
heated up a pot of chili, but it's getting cold on
the stove now. I haven't bothered eating because
Grandma and I made brownies this afternoon,
and I'm still full.

*Things here are the same as always...*I could use the same line in my letter back to Aracely. My parents still work too much and don't rest enough. My grandmother and I still spend tons of time together, cycling, working in her garden and baking stuff. Emily and I go to movies, and I hang out at the bike shop. (Emily's less scornful of my dirty fingernails now that she knows about Nerick, I notice. *That hot guy?* she asked, stabbing a finger at the photo my parents took right before we left. I'm in the middle, wearing the yellow tie-dye and red plaid combo, Aracely and Nerick have their arms around me, and we're grinning into the camera. *Yes, that hot guy.* The one who still talks about me. The one I still think about all the time, even though I told my parents I'm not going back to Cucubano this summer.)

...with a few changes. I've got fifty-five bicycles in my grandmother's garage, and so far we've raised a few thousand dollars to ship the bikes to the Dominican Republic. Last night I was on the news talking about it, and my parents broke their no-TV rule: we all crowded into Grandma's living room to watch. Today one of the guys at school officially

declared me a wack-job, and I laughed because I've never felt so sane in my whole life.

He frowned and told me I was just like my parents, but he's wrong. I'm trying to help people, but I'm not raging at the world and refusing to enjoy life. My parents have tried the deadly-serious approach, and I don't think it makes them very happy, no matter how much they achieve.

Collecting bicycles for Cucubano feels right, and the thought of Nerick and everyone else riding around makes me want to dance. It's about balancing the dancing with the doing, and checking that balance all the time. I know that now.

What I don't know is how the balance will look next summer. I can't imagine yet if I'll want to be back in Cucubano with my friends. Holding Aracely's letter in my hand, I think it could go either way. For now, I'll write back, tuck my words into the envelope and send my love. Sometimes, that's the very best thing a person can do.

Acknowledgments

Writing a book always feels like a community effort, and this particular effort began almost twenty years ago, although I didn't know it then. I'm grateful to HOPE International for the opportunity to volunteer in the Dominican Republic in 1996, and I'm grateful to all those with whom I shared the experience. Thanks to the Canada Council for the Arts for financial support of this project, and to Robin Stevenson, Holly Phillips and Susan Braley, who listened while I figured out what I wanted to say. Thanks to Ana David Emery for suggestions and comments on the manuscript, and to Erika del Carmen Fuchs for introducing us. I'm very grateful to Sarah Harvey for her insightful, creative and encouraging edits. Working with Orca Book Publishers is a great pleasure, and I count myself lucky to have a publisher with pizzazz; inspiring friends; and a loving, enthusiastic (and very patient) family. Thanks, everyone!

Michelle Mulder's favorite spot was the library when she was growing up, so it's no surprise that she studied literature at university. After graduating, she cycled across Canada, traveled in South America and married the Argentine pen pal she'd been writing to since she was fourteen. She is the author of *Out of the Box*, *After Peaches* and seven other books for young people. For more information, please visit www.michellemulder.com.